A Touch of Clay

A Touch of Clay

Maurice Shadbolt

OXFORD UNIVERSITY PRESS

Auckland   Melbourne   Oxford   New York

Oxford University Press

Oxford   New York   Toronto
Delhi   Bombay   Calcutta   Madras   Karachi
Petaling Jaya   Singapore   Hong Kong   Tokyo
Nairobi   Dar es Salaam   Cape Town
Melbourne   Auckland
and associated companies in
Beirut   Berlin   Ibadan   Nicosia

Oxford is a trade mark of Oxford University Press

First published 1974
Reprinted as a New Zealand Classic 1987
© Maurice Shadbolt 1974
This edition © Maurice Shadbolt 1987

ISBN 0 19 558173 3

Cover designed by John McNulty
Printed in Hong Kong
Published by Oxford University Press
5 Ramsgate Street, Auckland, New Zealand

For my daughter Brigid, as she grows; and for Beverley, who saw it through.

Contents

Death communicates to life the direction in which its plot unfolds and gives it unity and definition.

. . .

We can turn away and avoid seeing. We can rejoice that we still have the protection of our skin and bones. We can make our body into a shield, a walking barricade, and hide behind it.

. . .

I never know what liberal philosophers mean by the 'freedom of choice' they are always talking about. Do we really choose whom to love, what to believe in, what illnesses to suffer?

– ANDREY SINYAVSKY

1

October 20:

I COULDN'T LOOK AT THE CLAY THIS MORNING.

I wouldn't have looked if my father hadn't insisted. Even then I did my best not to.

'There,' he said, 'you'd better get used to the idea.'

The man and woman spread upon the roadside grass were quite dead. Broken glass shone everywhere. Specks of it glistened here and there on their bodies, even among their blood. The man's face had been damaged, but I could see that the woman had been young and perhaps beautiful. She lay perfectly still. Her face was pale and remote, her lips partly open; she wore a black dress with an arrangement of sequins on the shoulder. I couldn't believe that fifteen minutes earlier she might have been smoking, laughing, weeping, or trying to remove grit from her eye.

The people who had first come upon the accident, on that country road, were recovering from their shock and handing out cigarettes among themselves, looking over the wrecked car, the leaning telegraph pole, the skid marks off the road and through the grass. The cause of the accident wasn't clear. They might have travelled downhill too fast, or braked to avoid a stray animal.

It was late afternoon, and the hills around were dusty yellow. There were sheep and shiny poplar trees. The countryside had a glow of spring.

'Nothing to be done now,' one of the men told my father. His voice was shaky; he had a sticky streak of blood up to his elbow. We could hear the sound of the ambulance coming, still some way off.

'Booze,' another man said to my father, confidentially. 'They reek of it.'

'You know them?'

'Who doesn't? Mary Dennis and her fancy man.'

'Jack Dennis's wife?'

'That's the lady. That was her.'

'Christ,' my father said. 'Poor bloody Jack.'

'They been haring all over the countryside for weeks,' his informant said. 'You could say they had it coming, something like this.'

My father expressed no opinion. He shepherded me back to the car just before the ambulance arrived in a storm of dust and spitting gravel.

'Well,' he said calmly, rolling a cigarette, 'did you have a good look?'

'A quick look,' I confessed.

He considered me a vague sort of son; he also considered it his business to harden me, one way and another.

'Well,' he said. 'That's something you won't forget in a hurry. It never hurts to look.'

But it did, of course. She looked too young and lovely. And quite surprised by death. The ambush had come so swiftly out of the sunny afternoon. And the light still flickered in the sequins on her shoulder.

That was all I ever knew of Mary Dennis. I never learned much more of Jack Dennis either, other than that he bought and sold something in the town, was known faintly to my father, and had taken a young second wife. The fancy man who died with Mary was never given a name.

As for my father, the only other participant I recall from that diminutive drama, he suffered ambush himself in the south paddock two or three years later, while straining wire for a fence. A heart attack. I was about thirteen. And, I expect, sufficiently hardened. Though I did think it an unreasonable way for him to die, after crawling through cross-fire on Gallipoli so many years earlier. It was difficult to forgive him. That, of course, was even more unreasonable. And the odd thing is that of the two corpses I remember Mary Dennis better, though I had no reason to be angry with her.

Perhaps I am offering up my first love affair for inspection. God knows.

It never hurts to look? The trouble is I still do, though I do my best not to.

Certainly I couldn't look long at the clay this morning. If chaos is order unperceived, it was just too bloody imperceptible. I left the stuff satisfyingly shapeless and instead walked with Terror to the sea, along the leafy track I have contrived down to the water. This morning, a king tide, it brimmed shining about the roots of the coastal trees. It is still too cold to swim, or too cold for me. But the sea, while I sat beside it, soon left me pleasantly mindless. Not peaceful. Mindless. An animal quality. A beast without thought. And only the usual, functional needs. Eating. Shitting. Fucking. And a bit of territory to defend. A naked territorial ape. A collection of instincts. Fashionable. Altogether too bloody fashionable.

Terror, after a satisfactory shit in the sand, sat panting beside me. Kin, or near enough.

For we seem part of this estuary; that is true. I can think of it as an extension of myself. A scatter of houses, pleasingly few, arranged among trees along the shore. And the trees themselves dipping lumpy limbs in the water. Rocks; a stark headland with alien pines. When the tide turns away, there are pools, crabs, dead shells and mud flats. The marvel is that it isn't far from the city. Perhaps a dozen miles. A lost corner, marginally suburban, too rugged for the bulldozer. The treeferns grow lush. And the birds are noisy.

Rangiwai. Translated: waters of the sky. Or Rangiwai of the sylvan slums. Once true. Most parts are perceptibly more immaculate now. A substantial supermarket, satellite shops, a rash of well-groomed homes. In its upper reach. I inhabit the lower; the peninsula. A green and muscular arm of land among mud and mangroves. Still enough untidy dwellings with rusty iron and unpainted weatherboards to keep suburbia at bay. Such evident squalor should be nursed; our time could come.

I heaved my territorial carcass up the hillside again. Probably just in time. Before I asked myself, again, why I am living here; why I live at all. Which is one why too many.

Eat, shit, fuck. Get on with it. I turned forty yesterday. A decade up on Mary Dennis, at least. Yet still as likely to be stunned by the iniquity of it all.

Among the trees I passed my lifeless kiln. A week or two since my last firing, yet I could feel no urgency.

Then the lean-to at the back of the cottage, the wheel and the clay. I still couldn't face it.

Inside, among breakfast debris, I sought precedent from the past. From my grandfather's journal, to be exact. It has been regular reading for some time. For the most part it is short of fascinating, but it has its moments:

September 30, 1863: No entries these long months gone & small Wonder. The Winter past & we survive. An arrival from Dunedin claims eighty thousand souls are now upon these bleak Goldfields. The Dead, of course, might be counted in that Figure. The Boats are still arriving, with more from California & Victoria. They have heard that three hundred ounces may be taken in one day. They have not heard yet of July. How to count the Dead? It is easier to tell of July & the snow & the warm rain & the Floods. These Grim Canyons emptied the thawed waters upon us. Fortunately I slept on higher ground above the Arrow when that river rose thirty five feet in a night. In the morning the main Miners Camp was gone. There was a plain of Water. No Debris, no Corpses. Having selected no Claim, I moved on to the Dunstan in August, to Serpentine Gully. The Snows came Again. There were Fifty of us in our Tents. They said afterwards it was a Snow Drift upon a Cliff which began to move. But it might well have been the whole Earth, for great was the roar when it Descended. I was dozing in my tent when I woke to Cries of Alarm above that Roar, which I shall never forget. It might have been the Anger of God. I fled in what I wore. Luckily as late-comer I was on the Outskirts of the Camp & for that reason had room to run. We numbered Nine, the survivors. We look back upon the Camp but there was just a small Mountain of Snow & Silence. I shall never forget that Silence either. Last Sunday in a gorge not far from here the Spring Thaw uncovered a young couple in Frosty embrace who had lost their way while looking for these Fields. They were buried thus. I do not think this Country is a place for men to live long. Yet I thought Life & Happiness the purpose of my quest when I embarked for this Land & gave myself to the stink of Steerage & sickening seas but the quest itself has become Purpose & all else feverish dream. I am now on the Shotover, where it was said Gold gleamed on the hillside after the Heavy Rains. The Gold is here, but I need all I Win to live. Living is not Cheap in a place so cruelly bare. Only Life is cheap, not Living. Living is the expensive thing, perhaps always so. I scratch & pan at my claim for the Luxury of Living.

*   *   *

Lesson ended. If his journal has done anything for me, it has largely been to encourage me to begin this one. Yet I confess that mine is rich in entries transcribed from his; a kind of conversation. And a closing of the circle. Here beginneth and here endeth, amen; the mercy is that it has only taken a hundred years. Had it been longer we might have suffered illusion.

The clay wasn't so bad when I began to work it. It never is. The Luxury of Living.

I was still throwing when Tom Hyde arrived uninvited, presumably for lunch. Tom, among other things, is our friendly neighbourhood ecological fiend. The sound of an axe anywhere in the district brings him breathless. If Rangiwai survives bushy and ferny into the twenty-first century, it should in justice be renamed Hydesville. For the founder and first and only president of the Rangiwai Defence Committee. I sometimes have the impression that I am a committee member. A boyish and bespectacled American, moderately middle aged, Tom is also a rock hound, a contriver of currently fashionable jewellery and a carver of driftwood; he insists on me as ally, ideologically involved on his favourite fronts. Too difficult to explain to Tom that I just like the feel of clay. And that Rangiwai has reasonable clay within respectable distance of the city, along with properties at no great price and trees among which my kiln can smoke unprotested. I didn't feel I was buying a programme to salvage spaceship earth when I came here. Or repudiating the twentieth century, or the technological revolution. It was a matter of convenient compromise with what was left of life. Of, perhaps, avoiding too premature an ambush.

But, 'Instinct,' Tom says. 'Your instinct is right. It's becoming universal. A revulsion from urban insanity, conspicuous consumption, machine-made lives, computerised appetites. It

16

doesn't matter if this isn't conscious. The point is you've found yourself.'

Again too difficult to explain that finding myself presented no problem; not now. The fact that I did just that seems largely the reason why I'm here. Not to lose myself, either: just to understand what I am about. The clay is. I am. So. Perhaps the attractive thing about clay is its inertia; I understand that. I also understand that in giving it life upon the wheel, one slippery moment of glory, I make it perishable. It is soon inert again, fired and functional, ready to be shattered and scattered in a hundred rubbish tips. I understand that too.

Never mind. Tom stood there, silent, while the clay curled under my fingers. I threw my last pot of the morning and he helped me stack the shelves of the drying room.

'You've been working,' he observed.

'Just,' I allowed.

'It's still amazing what you do with this clay.' Tom, like others, is baffled by my insistence about using only stuff I stand on. I don't buy in better grades. Nothing alien.

'No point otherwise,' I answered.

'You're a stubborn bastard.'

I shrugged.

'Like your pots. They're stubborn too. Strong. I still don't see why you won't show.'

Tom is involved with a handicraft market. He would like me on display. A full-scale exhibition. Publicity.

'I sell enough.'

'I see a cult reputation coming. Pike's pots. Pearls of great price.'

'Pearls don't function, Tom. They decorate.'

'Sure. Why not?'

'Pike's pots function. That's their only message.'

'The hell it is,' he sighed. 'But okay, then, have it your own way. Again.'

We went into the cottage. Tom was quickly comfortable. I

looked out on the estuary while I poured drinks. The tide had been sucked away; the mud gleamed.

He talked about Rangiwai's most recent atrocity, or near atrocity. Five fine young kauri trees near a minor intersection had been marked for felling in the cause of traffic safety. The Rangiwai Defence Committee had, it seemed, won a victorious compromise. Two of the trees were spared; three fell to the car.

'Well,' said Tom sadly, 'you can't win them all. I thought I'd put you in the picture. It's developers and speculators we have to watch now. I hear rumours. Lois wants to know will you come to dinner soon. She thinks you're lonely, you should have a family round you now and then. She says to tell you to come soon.'

'All right,' I promised. 'Soon.'

'How soon?'

'Soon enough.'

'Lois worries about you.'

That, strictly, was Tom's problem. Lois is a jittery girl stranded among off-cuts of leatherwork, fancy belts, and a tribe of chaotic children. A long way from New Jersey. They came here because of fallout-shelter hysteria; they have been afraid to return because of race riots, war fevers and, more recently, pollution. Their lives are a litany of a decade. If Lois worries about me, it may be as good an escape as any. A relief from larger, darker affairs. And perhaps a problem not without remedy.

When Tom vanished among the fern, I collected my mail. Only one letter, from sister Beth. She elaborated on her usual theme:

'A relief to know you're more settled than ever, if what you say is true. All the same, I don't see the point of the hermit life, all this navel-gazing. And puddling around with pots. I won't consider you better until you walk the world normally again.'

18

All fired and functional, fit for use, ready to be shattered and scattered.

She added that she hoped to be visiting soon.

Lois. Beth. I needed only Janet this afternoon to complete the trinity of concern. And she came.

Janet isn't entirely my angel, but she is my buyer. It's not necessary for her to believe in my work so long as she sells it, as she does, with admirable efficiency. 'It's cheap and stark and simple,' she explains briskly. 'It seems to have some rugged appeal.' Big, black-haired and bosomy, Janet has some rugged appeal herself; I suspect her solid hips sway more than a customer or two in the direction of my pots. They are usually conspicuous on the shelves of her shop.

This afternoon, though, it seemed she was short. 'We've had a run,' she announced. 'When are you firing again?'

I told her the drying room was far from filled. She said that wasn't an answer.

All right, I said, then I hadn't been up to it.

Up to what?

Firing. Any bloody thing.

Why not?

I turned forty yesterday and besides –

She laughed.

'Jesus,' she said, 'I seem to earn every pot I get from you. You having doubts now?'

'No,' I insisted.

'You wouldn't want things different?'

'Probably not,' I confessed.

'Then,' she said, 'get on with it.'

'That's what I tell myself.'

She was getting on with it anyway. She had removed her jacket and scarf, helped herself to some red, poured me a drink too, and thrown herself on the couch.

'Despair doesn't suit you,' she declared. 'Besides, you've been through that bit.'

'Possibly.'

'And you've come to terms. Better than most.'

'Arguably.'

'So what's the trouble?'

'It never hurts to look.'

'At what?'

'It doesn't matter.'

'You've lost me.'

'I had a good morning in the end. After a bad start. I can't complain.'

'But you're not happy?'

'Not entirely. No. I thought I'd conveyed that. Do I have to be?'

'It helps.'

'Who?'

'Me.'

'That's reasonable,' I conceded.

'If you're going to be a textbook wound and bow type, strike a happy balance. Not all wound, no bow. I know enough of them; I even married a couple. Steel yourself. Launch your arrows of clay with deadly eye.'

'And look on the bright side?'

'Why not?'

'Pure Patience Strong.'

Arranged even more indiscriminately on the couch, with rapidly refilled glass, Janet looked puzzled. 'Who's she?'

'It doesn't matter.' There are times when I don't need reminding by Janet, or anyone, that I'm a dated drop-out. Janet can't have coasted past thirty yet. She and her kind drop in and out of lives and loves with ease, tourists from shore to shore, never bloodied by lacerating landscapes. No sweat at all. No sleepless nights. Or boozing binges. Perhaps just a bit of pot to soften the sharper edges as the years float greenly past.

20

Would to God I'd known how, or been born different or later. And pot, besides, doesn't do a thing for me; I can't buy that programme. I can't even, sometimes, quite buy my own.

'I still don't see why not,' she insisted. 'You love this place; at least I often get that impression. I even suspect, at times, that you enjoy what you're doing here. In weak moments, of course. I recognise my limitations as therapist, but still. Think of your weak moments. Enjoy them more.'

Soon, though, it was strength I was enjoying, or the illusion of it, between Janet's ample and enthusiastic thighs. Janet isn't one of your sexual tradeswomen with the considered and cultivated expertise of the permissive society, if that is what they still call it. Whatever the commercial consideration or consolation – still in working hours, after all, and in need of my pots – she is really just an old-fashioned good sort. God knows what they call the equivalent, if there is any, in these swinging times. Perhaps over supply has put good sorts out of business. Or into tricky and trendy disguise, like Janet. Anyway there was no doubt she most delighted in a pleasurable romp, country style, rather than some intricate adventure of the flesh. She liked to be taken honestly, if not in some unharvested hayfield, then upon the clamorous springs of my kitchen couch. With no more sophistication, in the end, than a Tahitian twist or two she picked up once on tropical vacation. This, it must be allowed, made for a colourful climax on my part, which she used cheerfully and fluently as fuel for her own. After that satisfaction we slid amiably apart. I wouldn't say that it had made my day, but it helped complete it. Among diverse thoughts darting through my brain was the possible proposal, to Tom Hyde, that a balanced ecology should provide for honestly functional fucking along with unfelled trees. Janet gave the shrunken substance of my strength an affectionate twirl and departed in the direction of my antique shower and grumbling hot water supply.

Dressed again, last drink in hand, the colours of our

ephemeral Eden beginning to disperse into the everyday, and her business affairs doubtless demanding again, Janet produced a large and disarming smile. 'There,' she said. 'As good as new. All right?'

'Indeed.'

'Let's call it a fond farewell from the other side.'

'The other side of what?'

'Of forty. It seemed on your mind earlier. If not now, then all to the good.'

'I see. Well, thanks.'

'And you will have those pots for me soon?'

'Promise.' Sometimes she can be too transparent. Which is nothing against Janet or anyone; I wish myself less opaque.

'Something I meant to mention earlier; I saw Anna the other day.'

'Oh?' I tried not to be interested.

'In the shop, to tell the truth.'

'I see.'

'Poking about. Looking, not buying. I had the reasonable idea she might have been looking for something of yours to buy, but she chose not to ask. And I chose not to inquire, lest I was embarrassingly wrong – or embarrassingly right, perhaps.'

This gave me some pain, I didn't want to think why. 'You could be wrong,' I suggested coolly. 'She's never shown interest before.' But then I couldn't help adding, 'How did she seem?'

'Gently vague, as always. But much better, on the whole. She seemed, I thought, to be taking more interest in herself. In her appearance, I mean; she looked more lively. More interested in things.'

This didn't help much either. 'Good,' I said, and wished I meant it.

'I take it,' Janet said, 'you still never see her.'

'No. It's not that she's made me unwelcome. We've once or twice exchanged most civilised words, when the need arose.'

'Then what is it?'

I shook my head. It is Easier to tell of July, Janet. It is Easier to tell of July & the snow & the warm rain & the Floods. I do not think this Country is a place for men to live long.

'Never mind,' Janet said, 'if she really wants one of your pots, she'll find my stock strong for Christmas sales. Won't she?'

'Probably,' I agreed.

When Janet left, I unchained Terror, and followed his twitching tail down the track among the trees. The bush still has faint colour of kowhai, but the shredded flowers are falling free, now that the tuis have plundered the nectar, to rest like golden snow in drifts beside the track; there was a cluck and a clang as a bird feasted on ragged remnants of spring above my head. Somewhere up the estuary there was also the sound of a chain-saw stuttering upon some presumably large tree; I hoped it far enough away. I tossed Terror a stick or two, to keep him interested, and myself distracted. The tide was returning, a swathe of silvery water across the mud in the late afternoon light; long-legged birds stalked its edge. I could have done without news of Anna on such a day. The Gold is here, but I need all I Win to live.

2

November 1:

THE SPRING RAINS HAVE BEEN THUNDEROUS. THE BUSH IS dank and dourly evergreen again, empty of the kowhai's colour; the vivid drifts of petals have melted from the track. But the pohutukawa is freshening now, with great gusts of tender leaf, towards Christmas blooming.

This morning, with Terror hovering at my heel, I walked farther than usual. The release of the rain's end. We have taken too little exercise lately. We walked the shoreline to the top of the estuary, where mud sputters out among mangrove, sandbank and sandstone, and finally against an edge of earth springy underfoot after rain. A thin patch of pine has sprouted here, with their needles lying thick around; there is the ruin of a hermit's hut, and an aged peach tree with a feeble show of belated blossom. The old man who lived and lately died there was the last of his kind hereabouts; he began as a boy on this estuary when the city was but burgeoning town still well over the horizon. He worked in a bush gang, picking out and felling the tallest kauri, and then rafting the great logs down to the harbour channel where square-rigged timber ships waited to bear them away. When the tallest trees were tumbled, he didn't leave for city work like most of his mates. While the fractured forest healed around, he stayed on for some reason, living lonely here, growing potatoes and Jerusalem artichoke, gathering oysters and scallops, netting the flounder which once flocked up the estuary. For money he seemed to do little more than sell odd catches of fish, and fossick in the earth for fossilised kauri gum, perhaps bleeding a live tree or two illicitly if that was short, since the trees were now mostly protected around Rangiwai. The city began to mount his horizon about the time his old age pension arrived. First weekend shacks, hardly more substantial than his own, began to rise and rapidly rot among the trees; then suburban homes of tarty taste bristled on the skyline. By that time the flounder were thinning, the scallops mostly gone. I yarned with him once or twice, when first I came to live here, hoping to find his secret, and perhaps his strength. But he was disappointingly short on conversation. He could offer neither secret nor strength, just a glass of desperately sweet blackberry wine, a seat in the sun, and a clutch of conventional memories boomed out in the belief that I was a journalist of some kind; he had dealt with such before. When he was carried off to hospital to die, suburban children pillaged his place, possibly in search of some secret hoard. If so, they were frustrated too. Now his hut is fast falling down to the level of the old Maori midden upon which he once built it. The last of his kind? The first of another. Salute. Terror pissed indifferently upon a wall with wild lean as we passed.

We followed an eroded old timber trail, half hidden under fern, and after steep climbing emerged at last upon the peninsula road, which would take us homeward; there was a pleasing vista of bright harbour all around, and the distant misty hills towards the mouth were streaking with sunlight.

The peninsula road is a single-minded affair, crashing through hump and hollow, and finally and sharply into the sea; it provides a boat-ramp of sorts. There are houses here and there on plots once savagely slashed and incinerated; the habitations grow scantier towards the peninsula's tip. We are retired mostly, we peninsula-dwellers: from active life, from active love; we pick up our pensions and watch tide and sunset. That is, apart from a boat-builder, a fisherman or two, a sprinkle of launch-loving commuters, and of course strayed urban refugees of unkempt and questionable occupation such as the Hydes and myself. I sometimes like to think the Maoris who once pottered and paddled about the peninsula, and likely warred over it, may never have had it so good; our wars and wounds are remote now, or private on our properties.

Terror and I had the road home to ourselves, not even a passing car, until almost the end. Then, out of the bushes, in bright and pied array, all shawls and jangling beads, walking sticks and bushy beards, I encountered the counter-culture in single file and surprising strength – five men and four girls if I could read the sexes right, nine simple souls self-consciously breathing the fresh Rangiwai morning. From where they came I could not tell: some bay or other, some decayed dwelling out of sight beneath the road and beyond the ferns. It didn't matter much. I supposed it was only a matter of time anyway. The communes had come. Or at least an advance guard, with a dazzling prospectus to propose to their fellows.

They nodded; I nodded. And Terror sniffed the skinny bitch trailing behind them.

So Terror had something to think about as we designed our day. Eyes dreamy, he twitched and sniffed and licked his crutch while I began to read.

October 2, 1864: I think I have never seen such Rain. I fear there are None among us who do not now Regret this journey.

The Madness of the thing seems to have no End which I can see. When we are not dripping with Rain, then there is the Wind off the snow to freeze our marrows. The waterfalls crash down all about us & sometimes we see the Wild Mountains through the Mists as we travel. All are strange & none have names unless we make our own. The Rivers seem in perpetual Flood. After the bare stony Desert which we left, an Eternity of hardship ago, this place should seem a Paradise of green things. Indeed the growth is rich wherever One looks. Trees & vines & moss & all manner of strange native plant cling & tangle wherever we move. Our feet slide & sink in the Debris & Decay this growth leaves behind. But where is the Sun? It seems it is not God's pleasure to let it shine here often. It is a place for Rains more Vast than the mind can comprehend. I think & fear our minds have begun to rot too. Our Fate may never be to reach that Shore which eludes us beyond these Mountains, but to join Nature's debris on the Floor of these Forests. That is the Truth for two of our Party, a week past, who were routed when trying to Ford a flooded stream. We fixed a cross for them, with their names Carved, on higher ground. For Christian men slain by this Pagan Place. Gold? They say there is much to be found on that Wild shore towards which we think we are making our way. Some took ship from Dunedin around the island to the new Fields. We were foolish enough to think it easier to find again the old Maorie pass through the mountains. But we have found only Mountains blocking our way again & again & Rain this damnable Rain & Death a sniggering companion at our shoulder. Gold? We shall think ourselves fortunate, should we ever reach that other shore, if we can find a seal to slaughter. Survival has become the only reason for this journey & I cannot bring myself to think it much of a Reason. Men must have more Purpose upon this Earth, or else we are no different from the Beast, running this way & that in Frenzy, waiting upon Death to propose itself, a Death which makes no more sense than the

Life it lived. I do not know why I find myself thinking & writing these things in this cave, with my thin Companions fallen asleep around me, & the World awash outside. All I know is that I do & wonder where in God's name it will End.

Here, perhaps. My ancestral semen, borne within shivering loins through those mountains, stuttered out inside a Victorian embrace, can claim this as end. This decrepit cottage beside a scruffy shore. This clay. This wheel. This kiln. At least I should like to think that my life, if nothing else, can write an answer. And an End.

I pushed my hands gratefully into the cool clay this morning. It began to thrash about as the wheel turned, as if seeking shape of its own; sometimes I imagine myself merely an agent, offering its ephemeral energy release. All a con, of course. A cruel con. But there is always a moment when I feel obliged to allow it the illusion of choice. Which cannot amount to much, unless collapse within my fingers if persuasion fails. Otherwise it is soon solid and shaped, no more to be said, another Pike pot adrift on the tide of the trendy market. And I reach for still more clay, offering it the same choice, the same illusion, the same fever. No one could say I am not fair. No one could say I do not feel for it. But I can take it as unsaid.

The morning tended to spring apart, however, when I considered myself throwing a pot for Anna. Not one she might buy in Janet's shop; one I would make as gift. This notion has overtaken me disastrously two or three mornings lately. For I am obliged to conceive of something in which sentiment, grief and mana might reside. At this point, predictably, the clay seems to protest. And my hands grow clumsy. It is not as if this experience is unfamiliar. Clay has limits; so have I. My pots might sometimes be seen as monumental, but that doesn't mean I can make a memorial.

On such a morning, then, the only thing to do was quit at the wheel; again. Instead I stacked the kiln, made ready for a firing. At least I might please Janet.

'We'll be all right again,' Anna said in that darkness. 'Just give time a chance.'

But time produced only men in white coats, nurses with quiet feet, and a courtyard with clusters of autumn leaves. It seemed there had been a faulty firing, somewhere along the line; I wasn't, after all, sufficiently hardened. It hurt too much to look. I couldn't look at all.

Survival has become the only reason for this journey & I cannot bring myself to think it much of a Reason.

This afternoon, just after I had begun the firing, Terror became clamorous up at the house. A visitor, presumably. Perhaps Tom Hyde with some sad summons to disaster; or Janet with urgent plea for pots.

Neither, as it turned out. When I walked up to the house, I found Terror holding at bay three or four of that tribe I had glimpsed adventuring along the roads of Rangiwai that morning. At first sight they struck me as some kind of deputation; they had a certain solemn air.

'Mr. Pike?' said one, stepping forward. The spokesman, it seemed; his face, above his beard, was pudgy and pale. With rather hungry eyes. Possibly older and certainly bulkier than the rest.

'Yes,' I agreed.

'Mr. Pike the potter?'

It seemed identification had to be complete before we ventured further. I nodded and gave growling Terror a pat of consolation; he quietened.

'We've just moved out this way,' he announced. 'A pad up the road. We thought we'd introduce ourselves.' He reeled off his name, which I didn't catch, and those of his companions;

it was all oddly formal. While I groped for something sociable to say, he added, 'We were wondering, you see, if you might have some seconds for sale. We're still setting up house, and heard you were on the scene here.'

'I see.'

Pause. We considered each other. There were still no judgements to pass.

'Might you?'

'I suppose I might. Down the back. You could have a look.'

They trooped behind me, around the house, in silence. But their eyes were eloquent enough. They contemplated most things: the terraced garden I had contrived with boulders laboriously brought up from the shore, the seashelled path, the grape vines, the paw paws and tamarillos hung with flowers and fruit; and finally the potter's wheel under the lean-to, and the smoking kiln. I led them to the junk shed, where a couple of shelves were stacked with passable seconds. Some slightly chipped; some chittered, patchily glazed, or otherwise inelegant even for a Pike pot.

'I like those mugs – ' the spokesman began.

'Take them,' I said suddenly. 'Pick out what you like.'

'You mean – '

'I mean they're on the house. Take what you want. It's just that I haven't quite brought myself to smash them up yet.'

'They look mighty to me,' he insisted.

'They're flawed. All of them. I can guarantee the flaws, if you like. But I shouldn't think that need deprive them of useful purpose. And at least their flaws are honest and obvious. Nothing to take you by surprise.'

Perhaps I stressed that point too strongly; I don't know. He looked slightly puzzled beyond that beard. And continued fondling pots, passing those of his choice to others, who echoed his admiration.

'I can't say how grateful we are,' he said.

'Don't try,' I replied. 'It saves me a problem.'

They filled cardboard containers with their booty; and we emerged from the shed. They seemed to feel it their duty to make more conversation, via their spokesman.

'A real garden in the wilderness,' he announced. 'I can see you've got it made here.'

'Made?' I affected not to understand.

'This place, I mean. So far as you're concerned. You've got it made.'

'Nice to think so,' I agreed.

'Think so? I only have to look around. The way you live. The trees around. The sea down there. And the quiet. The peace. The vibes. You must have it made here, man.'

He became most insistent, as if I were violating some article of faith. Perhaps I was; I didn't doubt we marched to a different catechism. He, of course, would know the good life when he saw it; the question was whether he would know life when he saw it. Beyond, that is, the excuses we arrange to live it.

'It's a functional camp-site,' I said. 'So long as I keep the rain out.'

But I couldn't say much more than that. Not yet. Not now. Yet they continued looking at me hopefully, as if I might deliver myself of wisdom at any moment. I was doubtless a disappointing ally, if that was what they wanted; I wasn't really sure, and didn't care to know. I hoped they just wanted my pots; my flawed pots. No more.

They seemed to sense this, to give them due; we moved back up the garden, past the house, and separated to the sounds of more gratitude for the things they bore away. I wished them luck, since they might need that more.

Afterwards I went down to the sea and pegged out my net in the usual position, at an angle to the current, between the dead tree and the mangrove patch; and waited to see what the tide would bring.

Since I do this for distraction, more than for profit, I

couldn't quite understand why I should feel so troubled. Then it was distressingly plain. I had clicked back into history. A curiosity. I stood in the same relation to them as the old bushman-hermit had to me; and I was, it seemed, as empty-handed as he had been. I had no secret hoard either. It didn't seem fair, really. I'd only just begun, after all. Too soon to become an example, or father figure, if that was what they wished. God knew. They presumably wanted – what was the fashionable phrase now? – the alternative society. I can't travel, or trip, so high.

Survival has become the only reason for this journey &

No. Every reason. I must believe that. Let them be content with my flawed pots, lest other flaws become apparent. Wading waist-high, I wrestled the net back to the beach. Black weed. Jellyfish. A couple of skinny flounder. And two small parore. A thin harvest for survival.

I stowed the net behind my boulder in the bush, and took this catch back up to the house. On the way I checked the kiln; it seemed to be doing its job without complaint, rising fast to full heat. In the kitchen I cleaned and gutted the parore, delivered scraps and scales to the compost bucket, steamed them lightly, then picked the bones clean for fish-cakes. Aesthetically undesirable, a shadowy weed feeder, often seen haunting urban outlets where the weed grows grossest. Again kin of a kind; and they made a meal.

There is, has always been, an alternative society. Of one. I don't have to believe that, but it helps.

When I'd eaten hugely, I took the two flounder up to Tony. My nearest neighbour. There was reason for this. Tony has just brought his wife Rose home from hospital. She has cancer. The pain has not been large yet; she lives without morphine, more modest pain-killers sufficing. And Tony can still tend her without vast problem. Both elderly, once schoolteachers through a dozen drab country townships, they retired here three or four years before I did. Tony wanted to fish; Rose wished to make a garden. It was too late for Tony. A year after they came a heart attack felled him for a month or two. Uneasily recovered, he found the climb up from the sea too great an effort, and sold his launch. But Rose made her garden. She worked on the hard and sour clay, fed and nursed it, until it crumbled finely between her thin fingers; she garlanded their cottage with reef after reef of fine flowers, and clusters of orange trees, lemons and grapefruit. They had a child once; he died in the war. No one could say they haven't earned peace. They have it even now. Since Tony brought her home, a few days ago, she has usually emerged in her garden, somewhere around mid-morning, and pottered among her plants with trowel and fork, tending things she will likely never see blooming, as an act of faith for an hour or two, until she tires. Then they sit together on their porch, with a large view of estuary and harbour, and drink extremely pale shandy. After a time Tony fusses around, fetching lunch. He enjoys this. For she has been fussing over him for years, since his heart attack, nursing him along, easing his excitements and daily tasks. Now he has the chance to show he wasn't so helpless after all. He had just been playing the game; now Rose must play it too. And the name of this game is love. It wears no devious disguise. When I find them on their porch, in the noon sunlight, I am unable to see two pitiful people contriving strategies to prolong their lives. I see nothing pitiful at all. I see young lovers. Tony fussing. Rose laughing. And the world trembling with light and leaf around them. If they invite me to join them there, to sit with them for a drink, I find it privilege; I also find myself an uneasily envious intruder. So I never stay long. I remember once, at some social function or other, hearing an apparently talented and feline female poet pronounce love a myth; an elegant fiction which serves to explain the animal lusts in our lives. It astonished her, she said, that otherwise adult people could talk of love with a straight face, that they could even bring themselves to speak the word. Well, I find it no problem. With no facial effort at all. And I find the word explaining nothing but itself, in the end. That is, when I sit as guest with Tony and Rose.

Tomorrow, then, Tony will fuss over fresh flounder for lunch; he will decorate it with lettuce leaf, sprigs of parsley, and slices of lemon. And that will be consummation. That will be no fiction. That will be love.

To call it a lie would be to confess oneself altogether a cripple. I may not yet be adult, but I am no cripple. Not altogether.

Rose had gone to bed early. Tony asked me in for a whisky. We agreed that she was lasting marvellously well.

'I couldn't ask for more,' Tony insisted. 'These last few days, I mean.'

I know that he has lately lain awake, night after night, in terror of losing Rose. But that seemed to have passed. He had been too busy treasuring and then plundering the hours, the brief time they had left together, before the pain began.

Every now and then, while we talked, he stood up and padded through the house, to listen to Rose sleeping.

'All right,' he would say, returning. 'She's all right.'

He made even that mercy seem a miracle.

Tony likes his whisky, and his pipe. We sat together for perhaps an hour, looking over the lights stippled upon the estuary, seeking subjects of substance which might take us away from Rose and her illness. But we never travelled far.

I said goodnight, Tony thanked me again for the flounder, and I walked home. On my way I paused and listened. Somewhere, not too distant, there was a new sound in the night of Rangiwai. Music. The beat of hot rock among the trees, breaking, scattering, becoming mere silverings of sound. I gave attention with mild and melancholy interest while Terror, slightly trailing, twitched and sniffed an opossum or hedgehog in the dark. We both relieved ourselves against a tree to round off the day; and finally both lost interest. The night could keep its sounds and creatures. I went to the kiln, and then arrived at this desk.

The waterfalls crash down all about us & sometimes we see the Wild Mountains through the Mists as we travel. All are strange & none have Names unless we make our own.

3

November 3:

IT SEEMS SUMMER'S HEAT WILL BE UPON US SOON; AT LEAST
that was the message I read in this warm and windless morning. I was tempted to swim. But the tide was out. And I had
to wait for the kiln to cool.

Anna. I still wish her name less like a cry. Better to say, my
wife. That has less resonance. But Anna she is.

Anna, then. Anna my wife. Of the easy years. Drinks on the
sideboard. Paintings on the walls. Candlelight on the silver.
Guests to dinner. Money in the bank. Life in reasonable imitation. Ask no questions of comfort. Ask no questions at all.
Bitter? Not so. Envious. I can envy myself and Anna, as if we
were other than ourselves. Which we were, once. A handsome
couple, they see, with charming child, in a home fit for fashion
pages, and sometimes actually found there. Mental pictures
swiftly frame themselves upon these unkempt walls; I no
longer feel such haste to grab them down, grind them underfoot. They no longer offer so much hurt. And, after all, our

lives were wholly decorative. That decoration is more a thing of wonder now, less of hurt.

Why not? Just give time a chance, she said.

Indeed. For egalitarian time offers all memory the same chance of rest, in the end, six feet down.

Those mental pictures then. My private gallery. Start with Mary Dennis, say, and proceed along the wall. Arrive soon, too soon, at Anna.

Again. Perhaps today I should travel past. For it seems time. Among this galaxy of images I can pick and choose: early Anna, vintage Anna, later Anna; private or public. I pick the public. That has not been my want before. Perhaps that has been my problem. Anna Pike, aquiline Jewish, former singer of repute and promise, who gave up all for her child and loyal lawyer husband. Anna of the beautiful people. That puts things, perhaps, at desirable distance.

And without a twitch of truth.

Proceed. See there Charlie, their child. Charlotte Pike, two years old, among sand castles at the seaside, or helter skelter in the waves, ribboned hair and generous smile, doubtless dashing to Dad.

The tremor now. I test myself tenderly against it. One day I may arrive at the other side.

Who is that, then, bending to sweet Charlie now? That woman there of richly coloured skin and moist sad eyes? Anna Pike again, no less. She pulls Charlie up to her full firm breasts; her black hair spills over Charlie's back. Together they shine with the sea.

It never hurts to look? God help us all. But try.

So look closer; Anna's eyes. There are parents, brothers, sisters, cousins, uncles, aunts, incinerated in Auschwitz and Treblinka in those eyes; there is lonely exile and lonely grief; there is a world of cruel wonder for those who care to explore; there is shy passion once made public in rich and sculpted voice, and now seldom seen outside her marriage bed. And then not often there. See, then, how she clings to the child; and her eyes wander, where?

Of course; to her husband. Proceed, if you can, to a group portrait. He is there somewhere, one Paul Pike by name, he of the safely reckless reputation, among the other house guests on the beach, the chilled white wines and the picnic spread. Rather obscured still, in that company, and not greatly distinguishable. His world is enough, hardly a harvest for the explorer. For it means all it says. He meant to marry mystery, with gentle glow of glamour, in Anna of the song; he did not reckon altogether on nightmares barely bearable in his world, when the ease he offered was not enough. Ease? Safety. Anna understood safety; Paul Pike was its name. And his country, of course, the country of the Pikes, a land articled to safety, immune from large upheaval and spectacular hurt, except that people had to die sooner or later, if not too often sooner; she knew what she was doing when she jumped ashore here. When she scrubbed the greasepaint of Pamina off her face, and stepped away from the dismantled set of *The Magic Flute*, falling into Paul Pike's arms. That same gregarious one there, of the group portrait, charming and witty among his guests while his wife walks lonely on the shore with their child Charlie. What does he talk about, to those pressing close, while his wife walks? Politics, perhaps. (He has mildly satiric political ambition.) Art, as likely. (He is a confessed dilettante, though with some genuine passions: those paintings, shelves of books and racks of recordings are not altogether for show.) His work, possibly. (Since he affects to despise it, at least in present company, he has a talent for cruel anecdote.) Or even sport. (He does not, you see, lack the common touch.) The subject need not concern us anyway, nor what is said: his situation, at that moment, almost says it all. Disposed thus, among smiling and mellowly drunken friends, he seems to say that life is there for living, so why not? Which, after all, is not unique. In demonstrable absence of answer, the question to be asked is no longer why. It is, quite simply, why not. Why not indeed? An all-purpose bridge, across any abyss; a philosophy fitted for any function. And perfectly expressed in his attitude and ambience now, if one cares to linger and look. Why not?

Anna, of course, is sometimes a reason why not. Other human beings often are. And that is reasonable too. We do not, for the most part, live our lives alone; we do not, for the most part, care to hurt. But even in the best of lives there is a limit to the suffering which can easily be shared; there is a limit to patience when cure is obscure; there is, to phrase it more fervently, a distinct end to the griefs which can safely burden a marriage bed. We can cohabit, that is, with too many dead; we can become strangers among the living, messengers from the pit. Paul Pike is familiar with that notion, though none would guess it now; he is no ghost at the feast, but plausibly the host, replenishing glasses much as he refurbishes conversation around when it empties of purpose or direction.

Who wanders into the picture now? It is little Charlie, pressing through people, clambering to Dad. And then sitting pertly on his knee. She waves cheekily to her mother. Anna, on the outskirts, waves back with gentle smile. Anna, it is obvious, has something to believe in. Charlie, her child. Paul, her husband. They are all she has now she no longer has voice to dispel her devils; they seem her strength on this solid summer day. The rest, perhaps, has been fantasy.

It is tempting to linger. To freeze life there. But it insists heavily on happening; on being life. So proceed to the next picture. A bedroom scene. Paul Pike, home late, lights flaring everywhere, his home a vast beacon in the suburban night, arriving at his bedroom door, pushing it wide, already fearful of what he might find. For that has been precisely decided. It does not altogether matter where he has been, whether he has in truth the smell of another woman upon his body. Even if he has. It is sufficient that Anna should have the possibility before her. So that nightmare, once again, has the upper hand. He enters the bedroom moderately drunken, for in drink he certainly finds guiltless relief from Anna's despairs and his own inadequacy, and a moment later he is no longer so; he has seldom seemed more sober in his life. For that is Anna there, flung face down upon the cover of the bed, unnervingly still. Those are emptied bottles beside her, with a last dribble of pills down the cover, to the floor. And that is little Charlie on the floor itself, in frilly nightie, sturdy little legs askew, a teddy bear crushed beneath her. Charlie has found her sleeping mother and, puzzled, sampled the sweeties scattered around. A stomach pump will save her mother. But nothing will save Charlie. The pit has opened up under their decorative lives; all goes roaring down.

There are no more pictures of substance. Just pale sketches. Postscripts. Each with ghostly touch of truth. A courtyard with autumn leaves. Quiet nurses; white doctors. And one day, in some rehabilitation room or other, a potter's wheel, a coil of clay beneath Paul Pike's faltering fingers. And something he understands. May God forgive the bastard, if no one else will. And if forgiveness isn't forthcoming, or God isn't there, allow him the consolation of clay. Anna, as practised survivor, may survive yet again. He has to know that he is a survivor at all, to begin.

So he begins, in more ways than one, this last of the Pikes. He begins again.

April 1, 1865: When first here, on this sullen Shore, we worked the Wild Beaches, looking for Leads of wash-dirt. But our Profit was poor, there had been others before us, we could only take what was Left. So we pushed back into the dripping Forests, following the Rocky streams, nursing the shingle through our pans for a few small Gleams of Hope, to where we are Now, another winter almost upon us. The months pass as if in Dream. We nuzzle like Wild Creatures into the flanks

40

of this New Land, as if for Mother's Milk, only we call it Gold. It affords us little Sustenance. True it is that Fortunes explode around us with much Sound & Fury & drunkenness in the towns of Wood & Canvas lately grown among these Trees. For men with such Vast hungers & thirsts find triumph too much to contain, when it comes, after long Hardships. They live wealthy for a night, paralysed by the perfection of Fulfilment, & that may serve for a Lifetime. There are none among us with malice enough to gloat at their Fall, when they creep back among the trees & streams & cruel Rains to begin hoping again. One gallant not far from here spent three hundred pounds on Diamonds for his favourite barmaid. We might as well survive for these moments, as for any other. None should begrudge him, None should laugh. Would it have been better for his Soul to carry his wealth away to the Towns & there invest it in Profitable Enterprise? No. He has what he wants. He has lived his Ideal. He has tested his Dream. Of myself I do not speak Much. I am simply one in this Common Enterprise. I live much as Animal in these wet tangled woods, with my Fellows, trampling through mud & Rivers, making our Camps & staking our Claims, shouting & brawling & boozing as much as Will allows us, & Sustenance. In this time I have earned less than a Labourer in the Towns, yet I cannot say I am poorer. No longer. For I waken from Lusts, from Dream, & know that I am but a Mortal Man as I look upwards to where the Snows begin to gather on the tall peaks beyond the Forest. I watch the Sunsets fade & know I am but a Mortal Man & no Gold & not all the Gold in this Land will cure my Condition.

Nor mine. A pity, then, that the youthful insight did not sustain him longer. It appears, though not recorded in his sporadic chronicle, that within a month or two his party at last struck a moderately good claim, as claims went, and harvested it through the winter downpours. With spring he took his share away, so far as I follow the intermittent account, to make life afresh on more hospitable terrain, the point of it all, his intention from the beginning. A promised land and life made anew; an old and largely serviceable illusion. So began the Pikes, amen.

And Pike the potter too. I am simply one in this Common Enterprise.

My mail box was empty; I was hoping for a cheque from Janet. But no matter. Things can never really be desperate again. Tom Hyde arrived on his weekly call.

'It's all happening,' he announced.

'What is?'

'To Rangiwai. This place. It's all happening.'

He didn't look unhappy. That was reassuring.

'Sit down,' I said. 'Try some red. Tell me about it.'

'New people. Haven't you noticed?'

'Indeed, Tom.'

'Young people.'

'Yes.'

'They've begun to arrive. In droves. Well, at least two or three lots of them. Taking over old houses along the peninsula.'

'So what else is new?'

'Jesus,' he said, 'you're a cool bastard. Can't you see?'

'See what? I've seen them. What else is there to see?'

'The fact that we're less alone here. People like you and me. With our values. We have allies.'

'Oh?' I wished myself enthusiastic.

'Sometimes I wonder about you,' he said, disappointed. 'I wonder whether you care.'

'I care intensely, Tom, at times. But I can't force it.'

He thought about that. 'Fair enough,' he said finally. 'I'm sorry.'

'Go on, Tom. With what you were saying.'

'Well,' he began again, only slightly subdued, 'the way I see it, this place is coming to life. At last. It's going to come into its own. It's been looking for a new character.'

The old one was rather the point; but I let that objection pass. 'And you think a few confused kids are going to do something for us?'

'Don't prejudge them, Paul. And don't look down from a height. The world's changing everywhere. Frontiers are falling. There's new growth under the old shit, wherever you look. Here too. The young are looking for honesty. The way you and I might have, once. All right, so maybe some are confused. Don't tell me you never were. And never have been.'

It seemed I might have to surrender that point silently. Paul Pike, ex-functionary. Once message boy for the monster, waiting on hire in a carpeted office, no truth under his tidy fingernails. Perhaps the problem is that Tom and I see different monsters altogether. He sees a selfish society without love or truth. I just see society, any society, as a functional fantasy, decoratively and distractingly devised, above the pit. Which plainly is my problem. My hang-up, Tom would doubtless say, if I could afford to share it with him, or anyone. For I can't. Unless to Anna, by way of clay. And that seems as remote as ever now.

'All right,' I said. 'Fine. I'll give them a chance. So long as they don't bother me.'

'That's pretty negative.'

'What do you want me to do? Strum up a welcome parade? They have their life. I have mine.'

'I'm just suggesting tolerance.'

'Which is what I'm saying.'

'Negatively.'

'Then consider negative tolerance as better than none.'

'You're a hard bastard to break.'

'I look after myself. That's all. I take pains.'

'That's it, then,' he declared. 'I quit.' He was thoughtful for a moment, then sat forward in his chair. 'I wish to hell I could.'

'Could what?'

'Take pains.'

'I see.'

'It's not easy.'

'No,' I agreed.

'It's Lois, you see.'

'I expected it might be.'

'I wish to God she'd take a lover. Or something. Anything.'

'To ease some predicament of yours?'

'Something like that,' he conceded.

'So,' I said, 'there we have it. And you had me in mind?'

He hesitated. 'It isn't quite that simple.'

'True; these things seldom are.'

'Company's her big problem. The house. Her work. Those kids. Also she likes you.'

'I imagine that's important,' I allowed.

He began to perspire with the effort of explanation. 'Another thing, you're a solitary bastard. A loner. You're not likely to break up anyone's marriage.'

'The perfect choice.'

'Don't take offence, Paul. Sorry if I've put it badly.'

I refilled his glass; it was impossible to be offended. His honesty was too boyish and disarming. He might have been enthusiastically approaching the problem of a balanced ecology. Perhaps he had been.

'I think the trouble is, Tom, you're asking me to play games. Real games.'

'It's not quite like that,' he said, faintly embarrassed.

'No? Then what is it quite like?'

'Well.' He paused. 'It's a matter of human relationships. Wholesome adjustments.'

'Same thing. Real games. I used to be reasonably proficient at them once. Not any more.'

'I guess I should have known better,' he said, depressed, and looked into his drink.

It was difficult not to feel sorry for him. Downcast because his friend wouldn't come out and play. I crossed the room and put a hand on his shoulder.

'I'd like to help. I mean that. Would a patient listener help?'

He groaned suddenly. Unlike Tom to despair. 'Nothing does. Nothing.'

'Then,' I said, topping his glass, 'perhaps talking about something else might help.'

'Like what?'

'Like a new threat to Rangiwai.' It was meant as a mild suggestion.

He looked up sharply. 'You mean you've heard about it too?'

'Heard about what?'

'It's only a rumour yet. One I prefer to discount. They couldn't be so bloody insane.'

'Who couldn't? What?' It seemed we were on mutually interesting terrain again.

'In the environmental crisis there's people who like shit-stirring. Starting provocative rumours. To see people like ourselves jump. In the hope we might be discredited, perhaps. Anyway, there it is. Never fire till the target is plain. I prefer not to believe it, for the moment.'

'Believe what?' I grew impatient.

'That anyone – even the dimmest fucking fool in authority – could contemplate buggering up the estuary. Using it as a tip, I mean, for junk and garbage from miles around. And then in ten years or twenty plastering it over with parkland to hide the horror.'

It appeared Tom could unnerve me after all. 'A joke,' I said. 'It must be.'

'Agreed. But still. It's so bloody logical, a plan like that, from the official mind. Who wants all that mud, all those mangroves? The crabs? The stingrays? Fill the bloody lot in. Get rid of our rubbish problem. Make extra space for suburban neuroses to be given an airing. Logical. In the logic of empire builders.'

'Possibly,' I said. 'But I still can't believe it. Ten years ago. Not now.'

'That's what I like to think too. At other times, though, I feel this environmental consciousness might have crested. Just a fierce froth. While things settle back into the same old disaster patterns. Who knows?'

'We don't,' I insisted. 'And I think we have enough problems with things we do know.'

'Too damn true.' Tom seemed back with his private pain again.

'So have some more red.'

He didn't need urging. An hour or so later he wobbled away up my front track. I settled for sobering myself slightly with black coffee and bread and cheese. I spread this feast upon the kitchen bench, with old wrapping paper to catch the crumbs, a remnant of readable newsprint which I soon was idly eyeing, for lack of other visual diversion.

It was no small diversion in the end. It was a sudden flame jabbed in my face, then a slow roasting of flesh; sweat swiftly dripped down my body. For Anna's cool face swam up, as if from some silvery underwater depth, out of the fine print and bold type. Anna, quite unmistakably. Anna, quite cruelly. It took time to disentangle the mesh of words which held her finely photographed features down. 'Anna Pike,' I read. And again: 'Anna Pike . . .' I grabbed for my coffee, anything, and the trembling cup slopped black liquid over the newspaper. Then for my pipe. But my pulse still raced while I tried to summon sufficient serenity to read further: 'Anna Pike, formerly Anna Lieberman, was announced yesterday as the National Opera Company's choice for the leading role in the forthcoming production of Lucia di Lammermoor.' Enough?

Not quite. I took fresh grip on the coffee. 'As Anna Lieberman, she was regarded as a coloratura soprano of great promise, under contract over some years to leading European opera houses, until a tour of this country and marriage here ended her career prematurely. She will be remembered for . . .' The print began to clog again. I had to lever words apart: 'Interviewed last night, she said she regarded Donizetti's opera as an enormous challenge – quite aside from the challenge of attempting, even if partially, to resume her past career. Asked why she now used her married name, rather than the name her voice once made prominent, she replied: "Anna Lieberman is gone, years gone. The past is past. This is a new beginning, without reputation, with nothing but what I am. I prefer it this way. Anna Pike is what I am." '

There could not have been a declaration more distinct, a blow more brutal. I began to shake again.

Then I quickly screwed up the newsprint and crumbs, delivered both to compost, and finished the coffee. Why hadn't someone told me, Janet, anyone? Perhaps it was reasonable to assume I read newspapers. Perhaps it was reasonable to assume I might be sensitive. Yet I might never have known. And could wish, at this moment, that I didn't.

I was still in huge sweat. And not just from the heat of the day, though that was something to think about as distraction. Outside, beyond my window, cool green fern framed a view of risen tide rippling. I could tempt my shaken flesh with thought of the sea, to banish heat, wine and shock. Like some primal consolation, an amphibian back to the watery womb. Jesus; I really had to get grip on myself again. Soon. Fast. Or it would be all downhill again. I grabbed a towel and ran from the house, down through the trees, Terror in full cry behind me.

The sea was gratifying, exactly as advertised; I swam out of the estuary and into the harbour, where I trod deep water and drifted on my back. All grew calm; all was sunlight and lapping sea. Again. Nothing but the slow tug of tide. And gulls high. Foster the fisherman pulling in nets in the distance. A shore glinting with the green of spring. Thank God for seasons. We might as well survive for these moments, as for any other.

Peace first; the world grew remote. Then mild but distinct elation with the day. I had, after all, a cooled kiln to open soon, beans to plant, lettuce to tend, a meal to cook. A life of passionate detail, if I could carefully compost the rest. It was mostly possible, and seemed so again.

Sea-changed, then, I struck back for shore. The land grew bulky around me again as I moved up the estuary, all stark yellow cliffs and shimmering shoals of trees; I idled into the shallows until a rocky lip of land nipped my knee, and then rose to my feet and began wading the rest of the way to the beach where Terror waited. He had, it seemed, made a friend in my absence. A girl. A rather pale sad girl in long limp dress. A stranger here. She was stooping to pat and stroke a surprisingly subdued Terror; her lank black hair fell about her face. She took no fright at my nudity, and it was too late for modesty. She looked, however, discreetly into distance as I fetched my towel from the branch of a tree, dried myself, and began to dress. Terror trotted towards me, claiming me as his own after all, with wildly wagging tail.

'I usually have this place to myself,' I said, if explanation were needed, while Terror licked my legs. I still felt cheerful; she was included in my larger mood.

'I just found my way here,' she explained in turn after slight hesitation, 'walking through the trees. I found tracks and followed them. And here I am. I found this little beach and lonely dog. He barked a bit, then I threw him a stick and we were all right. He's yours?'

'Yes.'

'He's nice.' She had a slow soft voice.

'A genuine mongrel; he should be a cattle dog on a farm. A misfit here. I bought a pup, you see, quite literally. He was

48

supposed to be a terrier. But he grew and grew. And the terrier became Terror. That's his name. For good reason, apart from being a misfit. He can polish off the milkman for breakfast and the postman for lunch. Very anti-social and territorially possessive, as they say.'

'Well, I like him,' she announced. 'We get on.'

'Good.' There wasn't much more I could say.

'This land is yours?' she asked.

'Technically, yes.'

'What's that mean?'

'I mean I own a piece of paper to say it's mine.'

'So you do, then,' she said, puzzled. 'You do own this place.'

'Or it owns me, for the moment. That may be more accurate.'

'I see,' she said, still slightly blank. 'I'm sorry if I upset you. I was only trying to ask if you minded me trespassing.'

'Of course not.'

'I just found tracks and followed them.'

'Which is all most of us do, to get anywhere.'

'Yes.' A thoughtful girl, quiet enough, unobjectionable. At least I couldn't much resent her presence here; she didn't need to throw me a stick. I didn't even bark. Perhaps I was now grateful for any diversion in my day.

'And where did these tracks begin?' I asked.

'Back there.' She made a vague gesture towards the trees. 'Somewhere; it's hard to say.'

'Hardly in the city.' For that was where she appeared to point. And she seemed something surfaced from alleys and lanes, boutiques and coffee houses and record bars, in that languid costume.

'No. I'm living near.'

'I see.'

'There's a crowd of us in a house.'

'I get the picture now.' Indeed; I'd forgotten. The new

people. The sea had briefly banished the conversation with Tom too.

'I'm just finding where we are.' She corrected herself, finding the fashionable phrase to fit. 'Where we're at.' She wasn't quite up with the play, not yet, but that no doubt was only a matter of time.

'So welcome to Rangiwai. If that's where it's all happening.' I could echo Tom and show my paces too. No untrendy hermit he.

'I like it,' she confessed. 'So quiet. So green.'

'A regular Eden,' I suggested. 'Complete with naked Adam.'

She smiled anyway. 'I'm sorry if I'm in the way.'

'The intrusion's mine. Upon your exploration. Mark dragons on the chart. Pike the potter and his dog, beware.'

'So you're him. I heard the others talk.'

'The others?'

'The others I live with. We use your pots. The ones you gave away.'

She made that vague encounter vivid again: the wandering tribe, the hungry-eyed leader, my haste to be free. Her eyes at least weren't hungry; they asked for nothing but my shore. Interested and bright, perhaps too bright. Could she be high on something? Possibly. But then I was high myself. No longer on wine; on sun and sea and an estuary with ebbing tide. I couldn't complain or object if she had her own thing; I might experiment and yet surprise Tom with tolerance, who knew? But it was the day, of course. The singed and healed day. And this diversion.

'Tell me about the others.'

'They're friends. We share. The ones with work help those who haven't.'

'That's sweet. And you?'

'I haven't. Just now. I cook. And dig the garden.'

Where pot, no doubt, would blossom as the rose.

'And just find tracks and follow them,' I added.

50

'When I can. Yes. Today's not my day for cooking. And the garden's dug. That's how I'm here.'

'And all this has just begun?'

'Not really. We were together before.'

'Before?'

'In the city. That was a big old house too. But men came to bulldoze it down. We had to move. We were going to anyway – out of the city, to somewhere green and quiet.'

'Peace be with Rangiwai.'

'Yes. That's how I feel. We all do. We're people with problems, you see.' She grew confidential.

'Oh?'

'That's why we're together. To help each other, and heal. It was Frank's idea first.'

'Frank?'

'Frank Daniels. He's the oldest. The one who came to see you for the pots.'

Of course. The hungry eyes, the name I didn't catch.

'And he's the source of wisdom?'

'Not really. We just sit down and talk things out together. Frank says that's the only way we'll keep our cool if things get wild, or love goes out the door.'

'Love?'

'For each other. Frank says that's all that can save us.'

'From what, though?'

'From ourselves. Our problems, our different problems. The things that brought us together.'

'I take it these are pretty big,' I said, casually prompting.

'For some of us it's, well, shifting off the drug scene, if you want to know. Something that can't be done suddenly. For others, well Frank says it's lack of life motive, confused social or sexual orientation. Within – ' She began hesitantly to grope among the pre-cut phrases. ' – inadequate patterns of life style.'

'And love's the answer.'

'It makes – ' She paused, found the word, and grew confident again. 'It makes the new context. That's how we see it. I mean, well, we build new rituals, you see, upon our love for each other.'

I didn't inquire what kind. That was best left to imagination, if I cared to use it. Which I didn't, at that moment. Her dissertation had diminished my day in a way I couldn't quite determine; perhaps because I was too attached to words which meant what they said. But then again, the day was literally diminishing, with the sun sliding down the western sky and the shiny tide departing.

'I've nothing against love, myself,' I conceded finally. 'But just now I'm more sold on the idea of a long cool beer. That's an invitation, if you like. You might find your way home more easily through my place. Otherwise God knows where tracks will take you, at this rate.'

She offered a smile; I had nothing against it. 'I expect I am lost,' she agreed.

'That's unless you were wanting a swim too.'

'I did think about it.'

'Don't think. Grab your chance before the tide goes. Borrow my towel. Don't be shy.'

She wasn't. A minute later, stripped and thin, she gave herself tenderly to the receding sea. She shivered and cried out at the first chill of the water, then she rushed in, wildly splashing, with childish delight. For she really was quite young. Touchingly young, though I had no envy. And her figure, if slight, was at least neat enough. But pale, too pale, a thing of the city's more sunless streets. She emerged dripping and ran to the towel and her clothes. I threw Terror a stick or two while we waited. Then we all three walked the track up to the house. She offered the usual admiration, the predictable phrases, when she at length sighted my situation among the trees and above the estuary. I fetched the beer briskly; it seemed about the only demand left in the day. That, say, and sunset.

She sat awkwardly, stiffly, in the chair she chose. I placed beer beside her, and sat nearby to sample my own. There was a lull while we rearranged perspectives, host and guest, across the distance of two decades. Terror, after prowling the room for a while, collapsed finally and rather surprisingly at her feet, perhaps anticipating more affection than was my norm. And that was forthcoming; she stroked his head and tickled his throat.

I didn't see Terror as a useful conversation piece, though; not again. He'd done his time. 'So what's your problem?' I asked at last. 'You've left me short on detail.'

'My problem?' Her eyes could be quickly vacant.

'Your hang-up. What brings you haunting the tracks of Rangiwai? The drug scene, is it, or lack of life motive or – what else was it now? – confused social or sexual orientation. I'm trying to remember what you said, you see. And I don't remember you specific about yourself.'

'That's difficult. Do I have to be?'

'It might help with the rest of the afternoon.'

'It's no single, simple thing. Mine's a mixture, I suppose.' She could, it seemed, be reticent after all. Or perhaps she was still adjusting to the atmosphere, the house, this rather antique forty-year-old stranger with querulous questions behind his beer. 'I expect I'm, well, still finding what it is, and who I am.'

'That's important?'

'Yes,' she said, baffled that I might suggest otherwise. 'Of course.'

'An identity crisis?' I prompted gently.

'I think that's it,' she said uncertainly. Then she plunged and grabbed the frayed phrase. 'Yes. An identity crisis.'

She'd heard of that. I felt a surge of shame; I'd baited the hook unfairly. But she didn't seem to mind. I proceeded, then, with care. 'The cure might be worse than the condition, of course. Knowing who we are might be more a disaster than not knowing.'

She found that perplexing. So I left it.

53

'Never mind,' I went on. 'But who were you? Before, I mean. Before all this – this sharing and loving and healing.'

'Oh.' She seemed relieved. 'That's easy. I was a dolly bird, you see, in a big office. Just another dolly bird. I could show you photographs then. You wouldn't believe them.'

Possibly. But hardly the point. 'And what went wrong?'

'Nothing. Everything. It just wasn't right for me. All these men pawing every day. Pats. Whispers. It was too easy to be what they wanted. I didn't have to be anything except what they wanted. Until one of them let me down. He was married, you see, with children. It wasn't so easy any more. We were going away together and then we didn't. I still had to look at his face in the office every day while other men whispered and tried to touch me. The nights were worst. The girl I lived with gave me pills she got from her boy friend. That's how I got hooked. After a while her boy friend started being mine too. He kept giving me the pills and doing what he liked. One night I just blew my mind and went wandering. That was when Frank and his friends found me. They were looking for someone else on a bad trip, and found me freaked out instead. They helped me with coffee and towels. I stayed. I wasn't Irene the office dolly bird any more. I was just Irene again among friends. Myself. You see. With people loving me for myself. Is that so difficult to understand?'

'No,' I confessed. 'Not at all.' With a substantial twinge; she had, for all my callous questions, given a plausible glimpse of hell. Dolly birds might never seem the same again.

She tasted her beer quite coolly. 'I don't like having to explain,' she added. 'But I can.'

'Very well too.'

'Perhaps it's your kind face,' she observed.

She had to be myopic, of course.

'Or Terror,' she went on. 'I always wanted a dog, when I was a kid. Something warm and live I could call my own. But my parents wouldn't let me have one. It might mess up the house, leave hairs on the carpet or bones on the mat. It was that sort of house, in that sort of street.'

'Yes.'

'If ever you go away,' she said, 'I'll look after him. I promise.'

'A tall order.'

'I wouldn't mind.'

'In any case,' I added, 'I never go away. Never more than an hour or two; that's the most I can afford. I wouldn't mind being buried here, in my clay pit, along with the rest of my rubbish, at the end. But I imagine the health authority, or some bloody authority, would have words to say.'

'You know something?' she said. "You're not so bad. You're quite cool, really. Quite real. I don't care what anyone else thinks.'

'You must finish your beer soon,' I insisted.

'Are you trying to get me drunk?'

'No. It's just that you'll have to go.'

'Why? Have I said something wrong?' She looked dismayed.

'I mean that it's sunset soon.'

'I'd like to watch it.'

'That's what I'm saying. You can't. We all have rules – or rituals, if you like. And this is one of mine. No woman stays till sunset. Or she might be here at sunrise, or for a week or two, a month or two, a year or two. God knows.'

'And that terrifies you?'

'Yes,' I said.

'And I thought I had problems.'

'I have none. That's the point.'

'Know something? I don't believe you.'

'That's a matter of small interest to me. Rituals are rituals. We use them to keep ourselves together. As you were explaining, in your way.'

That seemed to silence her. But I didn't mean to hurt.

'I'm sorry,' I said. 'Come again if you like, if you find the right tracks. And you need company.'

'In daylight only?'

'I thought I conveyed that.'

'And alone?'

'That too. But you're safe.'

'I can see.'

'Just watch for Terror. He doesn't like being taken by surprise.'

'I'd like to see him again anyway. If that's all right. He seems to like me.'

'Indeed.' He now had his chin upon her lap, where he was willingly nursed. His eyes were misty, and his tail thumped with pleasure.

'So I might throw him a stick. Or bring him a bone.'

'Good.'

'I don't think I can finish that beer, thanks all the same.' She rose. 'So I think I'll go anyhow.'

We walked to the gate, Terror between us. 'Keep to the main road,' I suggested. 'Don't try the tracks. And you'll find your way.'

'Thank you,' was all she said, quite gracefully. She walked away briskly, past the overhanging ferns and around a bend and out of sight.

I had Terror to myself again; he didn't follow. Back in the house, I settled into the silences and began the business of drinking myself comfortably into the evening. Terror, draped across my feet, dreamed of lithe and lively bitches and possibly thin hippies. The sunset arrived serenely, right on time, quite spectacular towards its climax, red and gold with lemon trimmings on the trees. I lit my pipe and topped up my glass and watched the last of the day drip, glowing from the sky. I watch the Sunsets fade & know I am but a Mortal Man, & no Gold & not all the Gold in this Land will cure my Condition. For we just find tracks and follow them. And sometimes grab the tide before it goes.

4

November 11:

THE HEAT IS THICKENING NOW, DAY BY DAY; I FIND MYSELF
swiftly in sweats as I work through the garden, among tomato
plants and tiny capsicums, cucumber and lettuce, or when I
clear the track to the water, slashing back the fresh growth,
and cover the steps with shells again. I fast lose myself in
seasonal ritual. I swim every day now. And the bait net brings
a bounty of long-nosed piper, feasting off spring seaweed, fresh
and delicate for the pan. Janet complains of an insufficiency of
my pots for the gift season. She says anyone would think I
wasn't really in it just for the money, something I can cynically
say. No matter; her cheques are eloquent. And I prosper with
piper; Terror takes the bones. It is true to say, though, that a
week or so ago, after news of Anna, I threw pot after pot in
an orgy lasting not more than twenty-four hours, and certainly
not much less. But this was more to do with madness than
money. And less to do with Anna than myself. For in
the end there was still nothing for her. These pots, in coarse
array, dried and lately through the biscuit kiln, make no

urgent demand for glazing and firing. Tom Hyde, at least, might think them honest. I could yet, given certain mood, take a hammer to them all.

Today brought Tony gently down my path, on his walking stick. Terror gave him no more than a constitutional bark or two, and then sidled close for attention. They get along. Terror, come to think, chooses my friends. By his barks ye shall know them.

Tony came slowly, examining change and growth in the garden, poking with his stick here and there, arriving at last at my door. Rose was resting, it seemed; he had time to talk, if I had. We took beer on the balcony, in the sun, the sea bright below. And peacefully passed news of the season, the fishing; I promised him piper again soon. He seemed, however, quietly troubled. Rose? Evidently not the cause, or no more than usual. She was still managing and containing her illness. She might yet see out this summer, though it would be illusion to see it as other than her last. Tony knew that, and knew I knew it, so we left Rose alone. And at length he circled towards his concern.

These new people, he said. Did I know much about them?

Not really, I confessed.

What did I think?

Well, I said, I rather liked to think them harmless.

And that, it appeared, was rather the point; his concern. Tony would be the last to direct a finger at anyone, to begin unpleasant suspicion. But his fowl-run had twice lately been invaded, netting torn, eggs taken and chickens too. One incident was easy to forget. Two were more difficult. What did I think?

'Only that it's bloody lousy,' I answered. Tony and Rose, as pensioners, didn't have much fat to live on; their lives had always been lean. 'I suppose I'd like to think the hairy man.'

That made Tony smile slightly. The hairy man is one of

Rangiwai's aboriginal myths, dying hard. The notion that we have some resident fugitive in the fern, making forays into the urban fringe, has some romantic appeal. With more embellishment he might have made a tourist attraction, with safaris hunting him down, another abominable snowman. He has certainly served over years as explanation of many minor thefts and incidents, a gremlin to grab for blame when occasions offer. Some even claimed to have seen him moving murkily among the trees – largely unclothed, they said, or altogether starkers, with a mass of body hair and hugely bearded. Also evidently immortal, since he has persisted in these parts at least some seventy years. Perhaps longer, for it has been soberly argued that he may be the last survivor of the Turehu, the fairy people, said in Maori legend to inhabit these verdant hills and estuaries at the city's edge; the last of the land's old native spirits, sometimes to be heard softly talking from the trees on misty mornings. I can't say I have heard such green monologues myself, unless with whisky or a hangover. But it is an innocuous myth, if Rangiwai needed one; the hairy man, most miraculously, never swung roaring and rampant from the trees upon innocent female passers-by. Not a rape in his record. As a myth he observed decent limits.

'I think we'll discount him,' I went on to Tony. 'Besides, he never strikes in the same place twice. And this one has, the bastard.'

'I kept watch last night,' Tony said. 'I was up late with Rose; she was restless. I didn't mention why I went prowling with a torch. It might make her nervous. This morning, though, I started thinking. I thought you might have some idea.'

'Not in particular,' I said. 'Just in general.'

For I saw Tony and Rose suddenly, and with some protective anger, as inhabiting that old square world which some thought themselves licensed to plunder, if they could. A couple of square old retired musty schoolteachers who might sometimes, in the twilights of Rangiwai, be foolish enough to believe they had done something decent with their lives, and by their fellow men; who thought there might have been virtue in what they had to give in bleak and dusty country class-rooms, year after drudging year. And now thought they had earned some peace at the end. Fools. Idiots. Didn't they know of the liberated human spirit? Cool, man, cool. Didn't they know they had merely been shackling young minds? Right on, man, right on. As the edge of my anger sharpened I wanted to tell someone, anyone, of Tony and Rose in depression days. Labouring in a large school garden so they could feed hungry children hot vegetable soup for lunch. The poor bloody old deluded squares. Sustaining a sick society, too gutless to challenge it. The world is going to be born again. Cool, man, cool.

'I don't want to call the police,' Tony said. 'They can cause more trouble than they're worth.'

And just what you might expect of an old square anyway, to call in the pigs.

'All these statements,' Tony went on. 'And they're just as likely to put the fowls off laying, crashing round.'

'True.'

'Still, I don't quite know what to do. Except keep watch when I can. Perhaps they've stopped.'

'Not if they're on to a good thing. No. I'll try watching for a while.'

'Could you?' His eyes were grateful.

'Better still, we'll try Terror too. We can tie him near. Even our hairy man wouldn't risk Terror.'

That thought made him cheerful again. And Terror, at that moment, was rather lavishly licking Tony's hand.

'I should have thought of borrowing him before.'

'He's just as likely to put the fowls off laying too.'

'A fair risk,' Tony judged. 'At least he's not going to ask me for bloody statements.'

Thus we disposed of noon. Soon Tony took the track up

to Rose again. But my anger was slow to subside. There were bastards in the gates. Not barbarians. Just old fashioned bastards. One thing about bastards, they can always find or fashion an ideology to justify bastardry. They always have.

So I comforted myself, in the usual way.

October 1, 1867: Whenever I force Pen to Paper, as I do now, I find Myself agog at the Devious games Fate can play with us small Beings. One might sometimes reflect that Fate could find better things to do with itself, more wholesome & Decent things. Are we worth all this Attention? I think Not, but then I am in no position to say. Who should have thought ten years ago that I should ever be resident here, almost at the Edge of the World, since one can journey no further? I can still Wonder at it now & Wonder why I am here at all. No matter. One cannot argue with the fact of Fate. Here I am in this Country, this settlement – can one fairly call it Town? – of Auckland. It is a poor mean place at present. Muddy streets & mangy dogs & rotting rubbish. Not even capital now, with Governor & Government gone away south. And these wars with the Maories have left it sick. There has not been much Money about & the land hereabouts is hard & rough, swamp & fern & Bushes & Forests where men fell the Kaurie tree for its fine timbers. Men have much Melancholy about the future, especially those who thought this country might be one of Quick Riches. There are still Soldiers about, for the fighting is still not finished in the hills to the South, & Maories are showing their faces in the Streets here again. They look Sad enough about it all after their whipping & their Lands mostly gone & their Race doomed according to the best Authority. I suppose it is a matter of no Great moment that I have late become a Townsman, my Gold lusts mostly Memory, the snows & rains too. Would that I had never farewelled the Goldfields, for it is Iron, not Gold, which has been my undoing. This Colonel Rogers was a most Plausible Fellow, with his talk of making

Iron, according to his secret formula, from the vast black sands heaped on beaches to the West of this place. He could even show the rude Iron produced to his patent in the small Foundry he made. Much excitement. All he lacked, he said, was Capital to exploit his discovery. I was not the only one Deceived. Other shopkeepers too were entranced by the Prospect of becoming Iron Masters in this new Land. Our moneys were forthcoming until he vanished. Then it was discovered that his Foundry was all a cunning Fake for the credulous such as ourselves. Also Colonel Rogers was no Colonel, not even Rogers by name, but just another shrewd rogue bred from Sydney's sewers who had learned advantage in speaking Well. Doubtless Time will catch up with him but not alas with our moneys. Those of us so deceived now have much difficulty looking each other in the eye, ashamed of our innocence in so Bitter a Swindle. It has ruined some. For myself I find it difficult to live on Credit again & with Trade so poor I cannot see myself here much longer. Poor Fools are we all when it comes to Hope. I have postponed my marriage to Mary Bradford until I find myself in circumstances more fitting to take a Bride. She, sweet dear thing, cannot understand that Love alone is no sustenance for the Flesh, only for the Soul. She weeps with bitter Despair, & each sob is a Cruel Cut to my heart. It is all a terrible Misery & yet I am not altogether cast down as I might be. I never really saw myself as prospering & respectable Townsman with sweet little Wife. It was tempting Fate to try & Fate, truly tempted, has made answer in this Crushing fashion. In that sense I may not after all be answerable for my follies. I am just another plaything in a Land which itself is but jest of Fate & a jest clothed with the illusion that Life might be other than it is. Poor Mary. I could never persuade her to understand that, with her reeling brain at present & floods of tears, & never could I explain that I feel free again of mortal illusion.

*   *   *

Irene was on my beach again this afternoon. For the third time or fourth; I am losing count. Terror leapt up, paws about her waist, in enthusiastic embrace. And reluctant to be persuaded free, until she threw a stick. Perhaps his passion made my indifference more pronounced.

'Something's wrong,' she said eventually.

'Possibly,' I conceded.

'What, then?'

'I'd sooner leave it, if you don't mind.'

'No sweat.'

True, nevertheless. Why demean the day? The chickens, or what was left of them, could come home to roost after nightfall. The estuary shone with the traipsing tide; the sun was warm, and the green hills bold. An afternoon personally painted. Before I swam I unfurled my bait net and excursioned after piper, among the rocks where the green seaweed swarmed thickest; the sea rose coolly around my thighs. Irene followed, after a time, and took the other pole. In minutes we had a wriggling harvest on the sand. 'Out of sight,' she announced. A good day; two drags were enough.

'You must take some,' I insisted as the bucket filled.

'But I'd have to explain them.'

'Oh?'

'It's hard enough now, explaining where I get to on my own. Without bringing back fish too. Though I expect I could say I met some lonely old fisherman. That might sound harmless.'

'Explanations are necessary?'

'In a way.'

'What way?'

'Our way. It's our rule. Always to come clean about everything in the outside world. To share everything with the others. To have something the others didn't know about, it would be like, well, like private property. We don't have private property.'

'I see. And strictly speaking you've been breaking the rule.'

'Not very much. I'm not speaking too strictly.' She gave herself solemnly to thought. 'It's just, you see, these meetings with you aren't too real. They don't really fit in anywhere. I might just have imagined them. I never say where I'm going, or where I've been.'

'Why not?'

'Well, you're the one who makes the rule about coming here alone.'

'True. But what are you afraid of? If, that is, honesty is so desirable?'

'I'm not afraid.' She was firm about that.

'I wonder.'

'Wonder all you like. I'm not.'

'I think you might really like having this little bit of private property.'

She sat on the shore now, an arm about Terror. 'I enjoy him,' she agreed. 'And swimming here. If there was anything more to it, that might be different.'

'Anything more?'

'Well, with you.'

'Oh?'

'I don't turn you on. That's obvious. You never look like making a pass.'

'That's obligatory?'

'No. But if you had to, you would. It wouldn't be surprising if you had to. People are people.'

'Most wisely said.'

Perhaps my tone gently mocked; anyway she flared.

'See? That's the trouble. You sit a long way off and shoot down people who are only doing their best. It's not as if you even look happy. You know what I mean, all right. People are people, and that's all there is to it.'

'Tell me, then, what if there was something more to it, to your coming here? It interests me.'

'I'd do my best to be honest. I really would.'

64

'Like how?'

'Well, like saying what happened. What you did to me, what you liked best, and what I did to you. And how it all was, how I felt. Everything.'

'It sounds bloody prurient to me. Like turning each other on.'

'It's honesty, that's all. Honesty among ourselves. All together, open. You'd never understand it.'

'Probably not, as a dirty old man.'

'If people are going to live together decently, begin again, they've got to have honesty.'

'According to the doctrine of Daniels.'

'Well, Frank says that. Yes. But we all believe it. We're all hand holds for each other. Otherwise we drown. There's too much to drag us down.'

'That sounds like Daniels talking too.'

'It doesn't matter who says it, if we know it's true. We can see the truth around us, in each other.'

I was briefly tempted to toss Tony's chickens into the conversation, to see what happened to truth. But I couldn't quite see their relevance, other than as a diversionary and doubtless unfair debating point.

So, 'Splendid,' I said. 'I mean it. I never fail to see faith as an attractive working proposition. And just how do you see the truth in each other? How do you take these hand holds, or where?'

'That's our business. Our world.' She seemed to have that off primly pat too. 'Something you couldn't hope to understand.'

'I'm over thirty. True.'

'And bitter.'

'Well worn anyway.'

'So you'll never know where you're at.'

'Here, just now. A reasonable surmise, since I trust my senses. They inform me I'm on warm sand on a sunny afternoon, with a bucket of fish and a pleasant sea. In which I'm shortly going to swim, given the chance to escape this with honour.'

'There you are. You can't face yourself.'

'So experts once told me.'

'It's a pity to waste the world. When it's all we have.'

That moved me for a moment. For she seemed suddenly to have spoken on her own account, for once, with a certain surprising purity. Not innocence; purity. A bell-like note among the discords. With echoes elsewhere.

'Tell Terror then,' I suggested sharply and stood up, brushing off sand. 'I do my best too.'

With that reckless assertion I cast myself upon the receding waters of Rangiwai. It cooled any shame I might have felt about my abrupt dismissal, but there were limits to sunny afternoons. Sunsets, for example. She watched me dive, perhaps with hurt expression, but followed soon. We swam out towards the harbour, some distance apart, and then circled slowly back to the beach again. Breathless, we dried ourselves, and dressed. She was slower to dress; Terror danced around her, expecting entertainment, a thrown stick at least. The human silence ended; she could laugh quite attractively, at times. And her skin had begun to take pleasing tan from the season.

So perhaps as well there was punctuation at that point. Janet's voice, a serene enough semi-colon in my day, drifted down the track: 'Paul, are you there?'

At least someone knew where I was at. I called back to her.

'You come up,' she insisted through the trees. 'I'm not coming all the way down there.'

Which entirely suited me, in the circumstances. To Irene I said, 'Don't forget your fish. It seems I must entertain.'

'Go well, then,' she said gravely.

'I'll try.'

Janet's arrival, anyway, had saved me from asking one curt question, whether Irene and her friends had lately tasted poultry on their communal table. It also likely saved me on another score, from doing something I might have felt I had to, if people were people. For it seemed they were.

This was less evident, however, by the time I laboured up the track. Janet, who could only really be placated with pots, had taken stance by my kiln. Terror gave a growl; she was too irregular a visitor to be totally trusted.

'It's cold,' she announced, slapping the kiln.

'True.'

'I hope you're not.'

'Not noticeably.'

'What the hell are you doing with yourself lately? You're up to another firing.'

'Perhaps I need more conviction.'

'I certainly need some more pots. If I'm to have anything at all of Pike on the shelf for Christmas. Even unconvinced ones will do, you silly bastard. Get on with it.'

'Says the world, knocking on my door.'

'You must admit I'm reasonably patient, Paul. I'm no slave driver, or ogre. But I'm not up to being fairy godmother either. If I didn't chase you, we'd never sell a thing, the way things seem. I came out to see if you were still alive. I can't help wondering.'

That said, we walked on to the house together, among hugely unfolding fronds of treefern and young kauri with slender shadows. A fat wood pigeon, bloated on berries, lumbered squeakily overhead and settled out of sight.

'What is it?' she asked at length, inside, mildly relaxing with a drink. 'Anna again?'

I saw no point in defiant denial. I let myself seem to consider the question. Janet generally came too swiftly and shrewdly to the point. It was really a matter of rearguard action, slowing her down.

'It's possible,' I eventually allowed. 'Anything is.'

'But Anna especially.'

'Sometimes.'

'You don't have to talk.'

'No. But it's all right.'

'What's happening now is altogether reasonable, Paul. She just happens to be looking for her own life again. That's all. It ought to make you happier. That guilt off your back at least, and Anna where she should be again.'

'Agreed.'

'Or is that the trouble? Don't you like that? Do you need all the guilt you can muster?'

'I don't know what I need. Aside from a fresh flagon of red.'

'Come on, now.'

'I tell you,' I said. 'I don't bloody know.'

'Don't shout.'

'I'm not bloody shouting.' But I cooled, nevertheless. 'All right. Sorry.'

'That's better. Things wouldn't necessarily fall apart with a little honesty.'

'So I've lately heard said.'

'And I don't see why you have to make a religion of the way you are.'

'I can only take so much therapy this afternoon. Thanks all the same.'

'Well, you obviously don't want me to talk about pots, my lack of them. What else is there?'

'Politics. Sex.'

'And leave religion out of it?'

'Preferably.'

'Did that hurt, Paul? It's true. You're too much the monk. Hair shirt, suffering and all. Apart from the celibacy, that is. And you're near enough to that, at times, you're so remote.'

'Try me.'

'Not yet. You told me once you'd like to make your life a protest against – what was it now? – the why not world.'

'I must have been drunk.'

'Not that drunk. Talking like an ex-drunkard, perhaps, awash in sin. But sober enough, as I recall. What did you mean?'

'Christ knows.'

'Come on. I never knew what you meant.'

'Conceivably, neither did I. But possibly I meant that why not is born from the death of why. When we stop asking why, there's only why not. Anyway it's largely irrelevant now.'

'To you?'

'Everywhere.' I found my second tumbler of wine wonderfully warming after all. 'You talk about religion. Well, there it is, the new religion. Why not. Lately described as doing your own thing. Regardless. Like getting among poor old Tony's chickens. Why not, then. Do your own thing. Fuck the Tonys of the world. If really pushed for logic, show your arse.'

'Now you're simply baffling and bitter.'

'Not at all. I think I'm really trying to talk about God. But it seems I can't. One thing you can say about the poor battered old bugger, before we finally put the boot in, He made some kind of sense. As a functional hypothesis. Now there's only a black wind out there, where He should be. A black wind and mad meteorites. And why not. The first bad news is we've got an identity crisis, sister. The second bad news is we don't want to know about it.'

'Now you've lost me altogether.'

'Take my hand, then.' I made the offer literal. 'We'll walk together a little way. Just find tracks, and follow them. How does that grab you?'

'Poor Paul.' She seemed to mean it. Her touch was gentle, her fingers slowly covering mine. And then as gently moving away. 'It's really just making do.'

'Oh?'

'It's Anna's hand you need to take. And don't look like that. It's true.'

'We've been through this.'

'Not really. You won't let it happen.'

'For good reason, then.'

'Like what?'

'Like you. Those tender thighs, among other things.'

'Please, Paul. A real reason.'

'Try this one for size, then; a real stunner. I can make it with you. I couldn't with Anna. At the end, I mean. After Charlie. Not at all. Nothing, just nothing. She said we had to give time a chance. We did that, all right.'

My face appeared to become involved in my fingers. Janet's hand was cool on the back of my neck.

'It's all right,' she insisted. 'Now I know. But I shouldn't have asked. I'm a pushy bitch. Sorry.'

I regained my wine. Janet settled into view again too.

'All right?' she said.

'Yes.' I paused. 'Of course.'

'We won't talk about Anna.'

'No.'

'Come on.' She rose, then drew me off the couch, taking my glass and putting it aside.

'It's not obligatory.'

'No. But it doesn't hurt.'

I found myself fond of Janet again; it wasn't difficult. And the need was there anyway. It was still some time to sunset.

Tonight I took Terror up to Tony's and tied him there with bones and bowl of water, near the fowl run. He whimpered, rather baffled, when I left. The night was fine and dry, so I hoped he might settle soon. In my own house, later, I sat down to a drink and some quickly fried fish and considered to-morrow. There seems no reason after all not to begin a fresh firing. I never really saw myself as prospering & respectable Townsman, with sweet little Wife. And a pity to waste the world, when it's all we have. Or all that clay, at least. I can give it a chance.

5

November 14:

LAST NIGHT, NEAR SLEEP, I WAS JERKED ALERT AGAIN BY Terror's barking in the distance. I pulled shorts and shirt about my frame and sped up the hill to Tony's. Tony was outside too, blundering about with a torch. I let Terror off his chain and he plunged into the trees. He knew his way, his enemy. With no scent to follow I collided brutally with branches, then skidded down a bank. Terror seemed to tree something ahead. An anti-climax, doubtless; probably an opossum. I found my way through the tangled dark, Tony's torch flashing in the foliage somewhere behind. Terror's barks still announced that he had something at bay. Then, abruptly, I was upon him. A boot, likely aimed at Terror, caught me painfully in the crutch. I joined a dance of wild limbs and tearing teeth. I grabbed at a perceptibly human throat, and launched a fist towards where a head should have been. It wasn't suddenly; I was butted in the face. Tony's approaching torch then gave fitful illumination. Our hairy man was hairy enough, true, if a bit over-dressed since last report, in jeans and torn shirt; well bearded, though, and wild-haired. And youngish and terrified, almost entirely as anticipated. My second punch was far more accurate, if still short of satisfactory, for I tripped on a log and fell across Terror. In this small confusion our quarry fled away to the sound of snapping branches. Terror yapped and snarled after him, with some hysteria, but I'd had enough. I turned to Tony as he wheezily arrived.

'I didn't recognise him,' I announced. 'But it doesn't matter. The bastard won't be back.'

'If he was really desperate,' Tony observed sadly, 'I'd have given him some eggs. A chicken too. If only he didn't tear the netting. The fowls get out into the garden and shit all over the path.'

I woke this morning with pained and feverish flesh and slightly bruised brain; Tony's post-mortem whisky had done some of the damage. Thus I found, in foul mood, some primitive notion of vengeance; that one solid punch hadn't been satisfying enough. A confrontation was called for. I could open the kiln later.

With Terror, then, I stalked the road up the peninsula, the tideless estuary sprawled muddy below. Retribution and his dog, no less. I found what I hoped to be the right track, indifferently cleared with steps crudely cut, to the house of Daniels and his ever-loving tribe. A smell announced a corrupt septic tank, or worse; the trees travelled apart, and there stood the house, slightly crumpled on collapsed foundations, with rusty iron roof, unpainted walls, and a vast accumulation of old junk around, bedsteads and buckets and basins and broken bottles. A pristine slice of old Rangiwai. A rather haggard girl, not Irene, drifted past the side of the house; and looked up startled when I spoke.

'I'm looking for Frank Daniels,' I explained.

'Oh,' she said, as if this were in some way remarkable.

'Yes. Frank Daniels.'

'Frank? He's here.' She fled to the door and shouted his name inside the house. This produced murmurings and shufflings and lifted curtains, and finally Daniels himself, bulky on the broken boards of the veranda, then creaking down the steps towards me. He wore greasy khaki shorts, a string of beads, and a headband saying *Love*. It might help to believe it.

'Pikey baby,' he said, smiling. 'Great to see you.'

Perhaps those hungry eyes made me recall him as younger. But he was still older than I thought. More than moderately paunchy, when stripped, and with a thread or two of grey on his chest.

'Like to come inside the old abode?' he went on. 'You're always welcome here. Our favourite neighbour man; we've been grateful for your pots.'

'I'm not here socially,' I said.

'No?' He still smiled, though.

'No. I just have a few words to say. Then I'll be going.'

I wondered if Irene might be discreetly looking on, within the house. That pacified me slightly. That, and my breathless hike here. Daniels still offered his bland face.

'Go ahead. They say I'm a good listener.'

'A neighbour of mine's been having problems with his fowl run. It's been raided three times lately. The third time last night.'

'Oh?'

Loud rock began to blast indifferently behind him, roaring out of the house. I had to speak in larger voice.

'I'm just here to say that if you know anything about it, or have any ideas, pass on a warning. I'll get the bastard. Or my dog will.'

'You're not saying we had anything to do with it?' He was still immensely bloody amiable, myself considered.

'I'm just telling you that someone, very likely new around here, thinks he's been on to a good thing. Well, he's not now. He did me some damage last night; I'll do him more.'

'He wasn't on your place?'

'No. My neighbour's. I told you. Helping himself to my neighbour's property.'

'Well, we don't believe in that, of course.'

'I bloody well hope not.'

'We believe in sharing, not stealing. We don't believe in property at all precisely because we regard property as theft in itself. The words of Saint Basil, the patron saint of the communal and monastic life. We don't steal from each other; we don't steal from others. Because that's our attitude, that property is theft.'

'You're not telling me, then, that my poor old neighbour's a thief. Because he happens to have a few fowls.'

'Not exactly. No.'

'Well, it's a fine bloody line. I can't walk it.'

'We wouldn't ask you to. It's not easy.' His self-confidence was superb. 'And it's really for the young to try, before we're all lost.' With a touch of apocalypse thrown in; that was all I needed.

'Let me tell you about my neighbour,' I said, lest Tony become a mere irritant detail, a fleck of dust flawing the grand vision.

'By all means.'

'He's shared all he's had, most of his life. And all he's had is energy, a good conscience, and a schoolteacher's wage. He's entitled to have a few fowls now.'

'And I'm agreeing, surely.'

'I must have misheard, then. I'm also saying he's foolishly generous enough to have given away the things that have been stolen. If only he'd been asked, and his netting hadn't been torn. He'd have been a soft touch.'

'I see.'

'At his age, with his heart, he shouldn't have to prowl around with a torch in the evening. Because some no-hoper thinks he's entitled to help himself.'

'I'd prefer you not to use that word.'

'What word?' It seemed I might have blasphemed.

'No-hoper. It's not in our vocabulary. No human being need be without hope or love; no one is beyond salvage.'

'That's your story. You stick with it.'

'And let me assure you once more that it goes against the grain for us. Theft, I mean. But we can't be held responsible for everyone new around here. What's your neighbour's name, by the way?'

'Tony Banks.'

'We'll do our best to check around. If we can help, we will. Believe me. I should like you to take our word.'

'I'll try,' I said shortly. 'It may take some effort.'

'I'm sorry you should feel like that. Most sorry. I can see we'll have to do our best to convince you. To establish good neighbourly relations again.'

Nevertheless that bland face beneath the pacific headband had blunted the edge of my aggression; there was no way now of getting past it. What did I really have against him? Nothing; almost nothing, so far as Tony's fowls were concerned. I saw for the first time that I mightn't have been talking about Tony's fowls at all. I could imagine Irene still watching from a window; I preferred not to. And I also began to feel an ancient fool in the act of trespass. Clearly time to leave. Especially since Terror had started to strain on his leash as if he smelled someone familiar.

'Sure I can't offer you coffee?' he asked finally.

'Thanks, no. I have work.'

'Peace,' he called after me. 'Peace, brother.'

Unlikely. But I found it this morning anyway. In the cooled clay, as I emptied the kiln. I felt satisfyingly emptied too. At least I had Janet off my back again. I treated myself to a cigar for lunch. Peace to Rangiwai. Even, at that moment, to bloody brother Daniels. If I had a telephone, I might just have been tempted to call Anna. But that, of course, is why I don't have one. So I made another connection. Peace to him too.

December 10, 1869: My Journey begins to seem neither long nor Remarkable & when I consider this place at the End I have much cause to consider whether I have Travelled at all, since my End seems much as my Beginning in this Country. What has happened to my New Life? My hands have grown Rough again with Labour & my bones ache again with my Days in these Kaurie forests. There is no Surprise as in my Goldfield Days. There is just Day after Day. All that changes is Weather. Rain & mud or rain & heat & the tall trees always falling. What roar they make as they Perish. I can feel Sadness steal upon me when I Contemplate where they once stood, the huge cruel gaps in the Forest & the pitiful wreckage around. But there is not much time to Contemplate. One of these Camps is much like another. We move from Camp to Camp when we have won what Timbers we can or when Money is poor or the Cooking. There is usually a Boarding house of sorts, a hotel with Dead house at the rear where drunks are thrown to Sleep off their adventures with the Rum which is sold here. It is made mostly of Fusil Oil, logwood, Painkiller & Treacle & whatever other inspiration the maker has, providing all the pleasure of being struck down by a Hammer. We live in a great slab hut with thatch roof & Vast fireplace with always burning fire to warm & dry us, twenty souls or more. There is no room for one to be Different or Alone & Never touch another man's Axe is the rule here. Also never go out to work if a Lizard scuttles across the Track. The Forest is filled with Omen if one chooses to see & accidents strike like lightning Omen or no. It is no pretty thing to pull what is left of a Man from beneath a fallen Kaurie Tree, which I have seen twice & would never see again if I could choose. The Mercy is that I put more & more Moneys aside so long as the work is good & the logs are thundering off down the river to where the ships wait at sea in navigable waters. I can imagine my Sweat & Life going with them on that Journey, except for that Money which one day will Purchase me chance to stand again on my Two Feet, so long as I never fall victim to that foul Rum in despair or pneumonia or a falling Kaurie. I cannot Hope for much more I fear since learning to my Dismay that Mary Bradford was indeed to marry another & that the Light she was to me in these Forests has been extinguished entirely. The poor sweet girl could no longer wait. She explained as much in the sad Scented letter she wrote & said she thought I would Understand. She has my Understanding, if that is what she wants & all she wants & if my Love would be embarrassment to her now, which I cannot doubt. But this does not make me more free or Love her less. What does one do with Love when there is no way to give it & nowhere to rest it? This thing which some think Rare Gift becomes a cursed encumbrance to a man, which not even Rum could make lighter, if I were to Weaken & join my companions fallen & raving & vomiting in the Dead house on a Saturday night as the forlorn revels of lonely men draw to their close. If ever I see the Inside of that place I know it will Truly be the End of my journey.

I could, I think, tell him something of the interior of the Dead house. A century of Pikes on; perhaps fated to finish there. No matter. I should most like to tell him, at this moment, how clay grows firm within the fire.

Mail. My sister Beth again: 'I'll be seeing you soon. It's time someone talked sense to you. If I can't, no one can.'

I braced myself.

The beach. Though the tide was still dawdling back up the estuary, I found Irene sunbathing there this afternoon, when I walked Terror through the trees, sniffing and snuffling and casting matter with profound concentration in his choicest places; but he took even more pleasure in Irene, when he saw her. He romped around her, and they rolled across the sand together. Then she discovered some dignity, rose, and brushed away sand.

'You made Frank bad tempered this morning,' she announced.

'Is that unforgivable?'

'I'm just telling you.'

'Sorry about that, then.'

'He said you were typical of what we must expect from older people, when we tried to build something new and honest. Suspicion. Intolerance. Even from you, he said. Even from you. He said we must expect no allies, only enemies. But even so we must still turn the other cheek, whenever we can.'

'I see. And is that what you're doing now?'

'It's what he says he did this morning.'

'And what about old Tony's chickens?'

'We know nothing about them.'

'You sure?'

'Of course. Besides, we live very simply. Mostly vegetarian. Only a little meat, never chicken.'

'All right,' I said. 'Perhaps I was wrong.'

'It would be better if you said so to Frank.'

'If I get the chance.'

'We aren't the only new people around here. And because others are young, it doesn't mean we're all the same, or that we can be blamed for what others do. Does it?'

I sighed. Cornered. 'No.'

'So be fair,' she said firmly. 'Otherwise you'll always be bad news.'

'Is that the message you've been sent to tell me?'

'No one knows about me being here.'

'What makes you so sure?'

I thought I saw a flicker of panic then. A convincing answer.

'You didn't tell Frank about me?'

'No. Should I have?'

'Don't joke.'

'I'm not joking. I'm still interested in what you're afraid of.'

'I shouldn't be here. I said I was collecting cockles.'

'That's not what I'm interested in.'

'I don't care what you're interested in. I should be collecting cockles.'

'Then let me give a hand. I'll show you the best bed.'

'You don't have to.'

But it seemed I did. I took her plastic bucket and she followed me along the rocks, beside the muddy edge of the estuary, until we arrived at a cove where the cockles grew most plumply on plankton. 'Here,' I announced, digging my fingers into the mud. She joined me. Cockles rattled into the bucket in our silence.

'Thank you,' she said finally.

'For what?'

'For showing me where.' She paused. 'And,' she added, 'for not saying anything to Frank, I expect. I really thought you might have.'

'Never. I imagine you too, you see.'

She smiled uncertainly. 'You're making fun.'

'Not so. In some such place as this, where earth meets sea, life was likely first imagined; God knows. So we're entitled to imagine other things, surely. You said it first. Not me.'

'Yes. Well, I do.'

'Also, evidently, a place for rules to bend.'

'You are teasing,' she insisted.

'And what happens when a bent rule is discovered? Bent or broken, say. I'm not very clear on that.'

'Well, the individual punishes himself, or herself. By putting himself, or herself, outside the collective. Above it.'

'With guilt, you mean.'

'Yes,' she said. 'Guilt.'

'And you feel guilty now?'

'I try to. But I can't really. Just because I happen to meet a man and his dog sometimes. Perhaps I'm not really a good collective member yet.'

'And it's all left for guilt to do its worst?'

She didn't answer. Cockles clattered into the bucket.

'Well?' I asked.

'You're not fair.'

'I'm not trying to be. I just want to shed some light.'

'I don't ask you things.'

'No need. I'm what you imagine. A man and his dog.'

'Then I'm what you imagine too.'

'That's the problem. I imagine I see someone who says she isn't guilty, but afraid.'

'Everyone's afraid of something. Of being cold and alone. Of never being loved. Of lots of things. Like being dead too soon. You must be too.'

'Sometimes.'

'So, you see, it gets you nowhere.'

'Not so. It gets me to someone who's afraid of something particular. Perhaps very special. And it interests me.'

'That's all it's going to do. Interest you.'

We concentrated on cockles again, until we had as many as she could comfortably carry home. Then we walked back to the beach. There was a strong smell of seaweed drying in the sun. The sand was warm, when we sat there. Terror sniffed around us for a time, and finally crashed beside her with a sigh and closed his eyes; he still felt his heavy night.

'You don't seem to see,' she announced presently, 'that I'm just as interested in what you're afraid of.'

I ignored this. 'Say I made a pass now,' I offered formally. For the afternoon gave me no credible excuse not to try the truth.

She thought, then shook her head. 'I don't know.'

'Come on. You can do better than that.'

'Well, if you must know, it probably wouldn't seem too real. Like everything else.'

'You mean you might get away with it?'

'With what?'

'A bit of theft. According to your Mr. Daniels, property is theft. And anything with me would be private property.'

'Unless I talked about it.'

'True. In which case I'd be public property indeed; my entire sexual repertory explored in seminar.'

'It's not like that.'

'No?'

'You make it sound cold and cruel. It's not like that. It's warm and gentle.'

'So I have a deficient imagination. Never mind.'

We sat quiet then. Terror stirred briefly, then slept again. She stirred too, predictably.

'Well?' she said.

'Well what?'

'What happened to that pass?'

'Oh,' I said. 'That.'

'Yes. That. I think you're just playing with me.'

'I think it just grew sad and died.'

'And I still think you're playing with me.'

'It must have been talk of Mr. Daniels. The thought of him dabbling among our deeds.'

'I know you don't like Frank.'

'Not just him. The times we live in. The trolls and charlatans walking the night.'

'He's not on a power trip. You just don't understand.'

'I think I understand, all right. What I don't know is how he does it. My shit detector isn't programmed for that sort of information.'

'It's just what Frank says. Suspicion. Intolerance.' She hesitated. 'And yet the funny thing is, you're not so bad really. You're probably not much different from your dog. A bit of love, and you might give up barking at everyone you see. He never barks at me now, never.'

'And I still do.'

'All the time.' She put a hand on my arm. I shook it off in irritation.

'Actually, I'm envious. The simplicity of the thing. Large words. Life. Love. Like things painlessly packaged in plastic. Tear them open, and the goodies fall out. That's how it all sounds to me.'

'And it all sounds to me as if you don't believe in anything.'

'But I do. I do.'

'In what, then?'

'In clay and what it tells me. Which is that life's always fatal. And love mostly too. No capital letters; just scruffy four-letter words.'

'I'd want to cut my throat.'

'I play with clay. And see what it says. Less messy. When it goes into the fire it can't answer back. That's my power trip.'

'Crap,' she said tartly.

By which I took it that she had encountered something undesirably difficult or unpleasant to understand; and therefore unnecessary to understand. Thus, crap. Demonstrably. The world was awash in such crap. And in the laundered land of love one took hand holds. So tell it like it is.

'Crap,' she repeated provocatively. 'Tired old crap.'

'Possibly. But all crap considered it works as well as any other variety. And it doesn't bother anyone else.'

She considered that, then spoke in smaller voice. 'I'd like to see you work sometime. Is that forbidden too, like after sunset?'

'No. That's safe. All in the hands, that magic. You'd be bored in five minutes.'

'I wouldn't. Promise.'

'Be my guest then.'

82

Her hand returned to my arm, more tentatively this time. 'Thank you. You see? You're not so bad.'

'I need more convincing.' Tactically said. Tactfully too. For fingers met, then hands. There was magic indeed in the hands, if one chose. And one could.

'I don't mind trying. I expect I'm not the first.'

'No,' I agreed.

'Your palm's very sweaty. Is it always like that?'

'An unpleasant personal trait. At certain points of time. It makes added lubrication for the clay, for example.'

I touched her thin thigh. There was a tremble in her flesh; she grew taut, then soft, and I found what there was to find, and covered her mouth with mine. Terror, indifferent to the movement, slept heavily on. She grew still softer, and moister, sighing slightly as I dismantled her dress, and uncovered myself too. Soon her body had a great deal to say. A lovely little wild thing on the seaside sand. Her urgent arms worked around my head, then gripped my thighs. For I seemed about to enter.

'Just one thing,' I announced then.

'What?' She was baffled by delay.

'This is theft. Private property.'

Possibly too oblique to comprehend at that moment. Her eyes were wild.

'It belongs here,' I insisted. 'Nowhere else. You don't talk about it. Understood?'

'Yes,' she said. 'Yes.'

'To anyone at all. It doesn't exist. Promise?'

'Yes,' she said. 'Promise.' Then, 'Please.'

At least I allowed her to entertain the notion she chose. I entered swiftly, no more preliminary, to be tightly welcomed. Then, perhaps the delay, she began to come again and again, a brutal bonanza as she shook and wilted, shook and wilted, and dug fingernails in my back; it was astonishing. I seemed quite independent of the huge harvest, though technically agent in the affair, until at length the energy exploding so freely took fresh and fierce shape in my own flesh and became rather stunningly a mutual thing; something I couldn't have counted on. I flew fast towards a finish, flung frighteningly free, undone altogether in the hot blast, then soon and slowly falling until we appeared at last serene on the sand again. Terror still slept without a twitch, unaware of human heavings.

'Out of sight,' she said; that freshly familiar phrase. 'Right out of sight. I've never had anything like that before.'

'Good,' I answered. And hoped I meant it. Her body had a glossy glaze of sweat.

'And you?'

I had to think about that.

'Was it good for you too?' she persisted.

'Reasonably. Yes.'

'You mean it was just interesting?' A gentle touch of dismay.

'A bit more than that,' I conceded.

'Only a bit? How do you feel now?'

A shade too analytic altogether. 'Fine,' I said. Since understatement proposed itself as desirable, given the circumstances. These appeared to be shaping solidly about us again, as we cooled in the lengthening shadows of a leafy shore.

'I feel freaked out,' she said in sudden surge. 'I've got nothing left to feel. I thought it was forever. I wish it had been. Because now it isn't.'

'That guilt getting at you?'

'You would.'

'Would what?'

'Remind me. It's not fair.'

'You made a promise.'

'I know. I remember. Don't worry.' That quietened her. Presently she asked, 'It's not the end, is it?'

'The end of what?'

'Us. It's not the end of us? You're not just going to walk off now with Terror?'

'I can't carry your cockles home. That seems clear.'

'I mean for good. You won't just walk off for good?'

'Not this afternoon. No.'

'You're cruel.'

'Honesty is, mostly. That's why we need imagination.'

'I suppose that's the trouble. My trouble now. I know you're real, you and Terror. I never really imagined you at all, though I tried to.' She looked miserable for a moment. Then she tried to smile. 'But it's all right. Really.'

Her eyes were tender with some kind of truth. I could wonder then just what the hell I had done. I just play with clay and see what it says. Sometimes it says too much.

'It's all right,' she went on. 'I'll be gone well before sunset; don't worry. But I expect I'll be back again. I can't waste the world, can I, when it's all I have?'

She didn't seem to anticipate answer; in any case I didn't have one. Terror shifted, stirred, rose on four legs and stretched himself yawning. He looked for affection, decided Irene most likely to give it, and wasn't wrong. I dressed, and soon Irene too.

'I'll go first,' she said. 'He makes less fuss if I go first. And besides, I'd sooner. If anyone has to walk away, I'd sooner it was me; my thing.'

Before long she did her thing. Also I did mine, for a while, sitting on the shore with my dog, watching the tide rise to full, and then taking the track up the hill.

Evening. An empty and toppled flagon. A soundless record turning. I furtively test myself at last against thought of Anna. She is still there, of course, quite immovable. This thing which some think Rare Gift becomes a cursed encumbrance to a man. Better a scruffy four-letter word, old friend, and peace.

6

November 18:

RAIN. THREE DAYS OF IT, FEW BREAKS, WITH CHILLY WIND booming over the western hills, and the estuary a clamorous confusion of snapping waves. Today, though, began merely grey, with dispersing drizzle, chance enough for Terror and I to walk again, down among the trickling trees. The beach was empty and slightly sad, sand stripped from the edge and ribs of rock revealed. And great gouts of richly rotting seaweed, green and black, flung in high heaps on the shore, and making a curiously colourful carpet elsewhere where it has gathered intricately dense. I have begun to gather this seasonal harvest by the bucket, carrying it up the hill to fill my compost bins and mulch the garden. I did not see Irene or anyone much through the blustery weather. Just Janet, who called briefly and busily to pick up pots and race them into the city in her van. It has been no great grief, inhabiting the alternative society again. No mail either, and no newspapers apart from wrappings on delivered groceries; these are swiftly burned or crumpled into compost with the scraps. Quite harmlessly.

The rain has left my clay pit greasy, without drowning it altogether. I laboured there with sharpened shovel this morning, when the drizzle had gone, jabbing and cutting out clump after clump, until it seemed I had sufficient. Then I scythed tall cutty grass growing against the trees, delivered it to the incinerator, burned it all down for an experimental blue ashglaze. This done, I felt some satisfaction in my sweat. For the heat had made humid return. I stripped and showered, and considered the sea over coffee. The piper have begun to thin, as the weed breaks up, but it is time for the mullet as sharks, with warmer weather, hunt them into harbours; time for my smoke-house too. So soon I was tempted to the shore again, where I fed out the net while the tide crept up my calves. I left it there to do its best through the afternoon, flipped a stick or two to Terror, and said goodbye to the morning. If I convince myself I am happy here, it is at least a luminous lie when the sun ripples through clearing cloud.

Two callers then; the drought broken, though I cannot call myself grateful. Tom Hyde again, and Tony. Tom first.

'It's on,' he said, and pushed into the house.

'What is, Tom?'

'This fresh fight. This estuary business. The bastards are for real. I wish to hell you took interest in the world. I wouldn't have to explain.'

'Try.'

'It's all I told you. It wasn't rumour. Not at all. Down to the fine detail. They want the estuary as a tip for twenty years at least, then they'll flatten and grass it over as consolation. Park in the sky when you die. That's the shitty plot. It's been on in secret for months, and the pricks have only just unveiled it. So there's damn all time for objections, any protest at all. They'll plead urgency with rubbish disposal; they'll threaten chaos.'

It took time to believe.

'Say something,' he said. 'For God's sake.'

It seemed I couldn't.

'You're no help at all,' he announced.

'No,' I agreed. 'Probably not.'

'What are you thinking, then?'

'That I might have known.'

'That's just bloody negative.'

'Things change. Nothing lasts.'

'Of all people – ' He paused. 'I can't believe that you, of all people, would let it go without a fight. This last little wilderness. A junkyard, for God's sake.'

'Sad,' I said.

'Is that all you've got to say?'

'Also that I feel tired suddenly.'

And sick. Quite sick.

'So you'll give up?'

'I didn't say that. I'll try to help.'

'That's more like it. What we've got to do, you see, is use reasoned argument this time. No slogan shouting. Reason. Alternative methods of urban rubbish disposal. A pulverising plant. Recycling. The whole bit. Then the ecological consequence to the estuary. Fouling it up with poisonous seepage from wastes. Killing it as a breeding ground for fish, a pleasure patch for humans. We can make a potent case, believe me, given time. It's just that we haven't much, we have to move fast. Perhaps you could prepare our case this time. You're a lawyer.'

'Was,' I corrected. 'Once.'

'Don't split hairs.'

'I only have business with the one client now. I put his case.'

'What the hell are you talking about?'

'Clay, I think.'

'Don't joke. I was counting on you.'

'You can, Tom. I'll donate the cheque from my last firing to the defence committee. It could be around five hundred dollars. Enough to take on a real lawyer. Not one who lost his nerve.'

'That's generous, but – '

'And the cheque after that, if that's not enough. And the cheque after that too.'

'Christ,' he said. 'Don't get reckless. You have to live.'

'True. That's the point.'

'I see.' He still looked amazed.

'Only one condition. That you don't ask me to do anything else. To chair meetings, make speeches, write reports, anything. Otherwise you can have all the proceeds I can soak from my present client. He might only be an excuse for living the way I do anyway.'

'You're an answer to a prayer. The second answer this morning. We've got manpower and now money too; we're away. I met this guy Daniels on my way down here, you see. Frank Daniels. Seems to know you.'

'Yes,' I admitted.

'Seems helpful. I mentioned our problem. He promised the backing of his people. To run messages, picket, do any donkey work. Very agreeable. Strong on ecology anyway, which is what we want.' He stood up. 'I must move. A lot of calls to make this morning.'

'You haven't mentioned your problem.'

'I've told you everything.'

'The other one. The personal one.'

'Oh,' he said. 'That. Lois and I are all right again, I guess. We're over the hump. No sweat, in the end. But she still wants to know when you're coming to dinner. Is it any use asking?'

'Soon,' I promised.

'I must run,' Tom said.

I was in sudden mood to run too. I could have done without his visit. But I couldn't do without the estuary. I went outside for a while, Terror tagging behind, treading my shaky acres cautiously; it was all I could do to look down on the sea. The sun was dazzling on the water. And perhaps the net was filling with fish. I got back to the house and found Tony.

'The day's come right,' he observed. 'Your beans away?'

'I'll be staking them soon. The tomatoes are slow. The bugs seem around early.'

'The rain won't hurt anyway.'

'No.'

A pause. Tony with something on his mind again.

'How's Rose?' I asked.

Not that anyway. He had to consider.

'She had a good night. Amazing, when you think. Three months ago, in hospital, I wouldn't have given her another week. And now, she's almost herself. Weak, that's all. They tell me there are sometimes quite remarkable remissions. Doctors can't quite explain. Miracles, more or less.'

I didn't look into his eyes, lest I saw too much hope hovering there. So I suggested, 'Love, Tony. Common garden love without bugs. No miracle.'

He was embarrassed. 'I do my best,' he said. 'It's a precious summer, whatever happens.'

For that reason, then, I decided against telling Tony about the estuary. If he didn't know, I wouldn't be the one to bring bad news. He and Rose might take pleasure in the tree-fringed tides a little longer this last summer. Please God they could, without pain.

'I thought you might be interested in some news,' Tony went on. 'I had another visitor.'

'Last night?'

'No. A daytime one, this fellow. And he didn't take anything.'

'I see,' I said, waiting.

'A Mr. Daniels.'

I might have known. The bastard was infiltrating everywhere. The future squire of Rangiwai.

'Seemed reasonable to me,' Tony continued. 'A bit way out,

but I could follow most of what he said. He wanted me to know that his people, his group or whatever they are, had nothing to do with these raids on my fowl run. He was upset that anyone should think they might be stealing. Very earnest, he was. Very.'

'I can imagine,' I said. For I could.

'I tried to put his mind at rest. I said we didn't blame anyone specially. And certainly not his people. But he insisted rumour had come his way. And wanted to put things right.'

'So he did, as far as you're concerned?'

'Oh he did, all right. He had a couple of friends along with him, young fellows. And they all set about mending things for me, putting up fresh netting. They said they'd keep an eye open for me, if I liked. I told them that wasn't necessary now. They couldn't have been more obliging, altogether. This Daniels talked a lot. Interesting. Unusual ideas. The future is communal, he says. People helping and loving each other. And this, helping me, was just putting it into practice.'

'A trial run?'

'More or less. It bowled me over. Rose wondered what on earth was going on. I tried to get into the spirit of the thing. I couldn't let them do all that for me without some thanks. I gave them a couple of dozen eggs and a chicken for Sunday dinner. What puzzles me is their turning up here at all. It's hard to explain.'

Not really. I'd given Tony's name. And said he'd be a soft touch, now presumably confirmed. Also they were safe, now, from any pestering police. I didn't say anything to Tony, though. There was no virtue in sharing cynicism. He could polish the little mystery to pass his days, warm himself with wonder. Who could it hurt?

'You haven't said much,' Tony observed finally.

'No.'

'Even at my age life still has some surprises after all. If you can't be surprised, I expect, you might as well be dead.'

'Probably,' I agreed.

It seemed I was thinking of Irene, though I should have preferred otherwise. It was easier when Tony talked again of gardens in the season's sun.

Easier elsewhere too.

January 14, 1872: Summer with us once more with blazing Sun & long Twilights & Time at last to resume this Journal, abandoned these many Months past while I have been busy becoming again my own industrious Master. Fortune can wear most Enigmatic smile, as I have been slow to learn, but what a Merry Dance is life as we turn to its tune. For here I am now seeking not the live Kaurie, but the dead. The Giants I work among are not those which topple Vastly with tall crowns crashing, no Longer. I cannot say I have regret. I work instead, my own man, among the great graveyards of ancient fallen forest which occupy the northern parts of these Islands. I am told it is hundreds perhaps thousands of years since these trees Perished & left behind a wealth of Fossil gum which has much use for Industrial Purpose such as hard drying Varnishes, this value only discovered as of Late, the Maories using it only as Timber Fuel. Thus a most Profitable Trade has opened up, with much chance for those with Eye to the Future. So I am no longer in that gloomy wet Forest which once seemed impossible of Escape, a leafy Prison with Drunken inmates, but instead upon these Plains & Valleys open to the Sun. It is true there is no great Beauty here. These forest graveyards have altogether a most Drear & monotonous aspect in all directions with nothing much but low scrub & coarse grasses & a little Fern & Bracken sprouting from the hard Clay. One would never Dream that this was once a Verdant Place of tall trees & rabid green growth in Ancient Time before men walked here. Summer brings but aromatic smell to the scrub or tea tree as some call it & pale flower flooding forth upon the hillsides like unseasonal Snow, which in truth is unknown in these warmer parts. Even then one cannot call the place Sightly.

Yet this said I must also say or confess that it can make my Heart rejoice as I gaze upon it, cherishing my Freedom again in a place which some might call the End of the World, but which for me seems Beginning after all. My Companions here who also scrabble for this Gum are mostly men of Independence with pasts & Griefs behind them. Some have tried the Gold too & some the miserable Employment offering in the Towns & some have borne Arms in the wars against the Maories & some have Deserted vessels with hard Masters. There are in truth all manner of Men without Masters & Women to drive them. Americans from California who took ship here for new Frontier places, a Frenchman or two, a Finn & some Swedes, Germans, Irish, & of course some Maories who have begun to see the Value of money in the stuff they formerly burned & took for granted. Also prominent & beginning to arrive in greater Number are these Austrians, although most are not Proud to call themselves Such, having fled military service for their Empire from their Southern provinces by the Mediterranean, Serbia & Croatia & Dalmatia & like troublesome places.

One of these a Dalmatian by origin is my neighbour & a first comer on this field & hopes one day to bring his wife too to share his Lonely life here. He has meantime made himself Comfortable enough with arum lilies growing at the door of his little Sod hut, & even a grape vine or two beginning to bear behind. We pass conversation sometimes in these long Summer evenings, even if his English is not much, while we scrape & clean the clay from our daily harvests of Gum for the Buyers. It helps pass the time of the tedious Task & makes his English better. He tells me as best he can of his Visions here. He sees all this Land as something sour which Man will yet sweeten with his sweat so all manner of things will bloom & fruit, gardens & orchards & pastures & vineyards, & where families will flourish in Peace & everlasting Happiness with New Life far from the Strifes & miseries & cruelties of older places. It is far from unpleasant thinking & kin to my own Dream if at time difficult to hold to as we go about our Daily Task in the hot sun which Truth to tell is as sometimes as Fierce as any the Tropics know.

When the surface Gum is gathered, as it mostly is now, then one must look beneath the Clay to extract this tough Treasure. One must use the Eye carefully to see where some great tree has fallen, the bulge in the ground thrown up by the roots, then pace out some Sixty or Seventy feet in the direction where the Trunk may have Travelled. There if one is Fortunate one will find Gum collected in the long rotted forks of the Vanished tree. There is only the gum left to tell of the Giant that was, the amber Essence of Primeval Times. But there is small chance to reflect thus as one Embarks on the task of discovering & retrieving it. The method devised for this in swampier parts is Ingenious, an implement not unlike a spear which is jabbed into the clay until something solid is encountered of the Desired Consistency, learned by instinct, which is the gum we seek. There only remains then to trench the area & take all one can Find & then carry it home sometimes miles through rude tracks winding among the Hills to where our huts are, no Small Task either before Dark falls upon the Visage of this Land.

As the smoke from our fires curls against the Sunset & my neighbour talks his Visions while we scrape & clean our Winnings of the day, I sometimes think of those who will inhabit that Glowing Future a century hence, my own descendants perhaps if I leave any here. Will they never remember us, our ordinary toils & troubles & Trials in these times when their Land was begun? Or shall they be too fervently Engaged upon that happiness which our Labours have provided? Yet I like to think of some Future Pike paused in his day wondering what this miserable Ancestor hath wrought here & thinking that his Ancestor might have been more than that merely but also a man with faltering Fires in his belly & fear of God in his brain and Lust in his loins & aches in his Arms. It is not Respect I would wish from him that future Pike a century or two hence or Gratitude either but just a Memory that I was here also upon God's earth once & a man like him who worked & suffered & loved to small avail in this Land where I still try to plant my Roots. I should not begrudge him all his Happiness if he should remember that I once was here too & take strength from the Knowledge perhaps. Otherwise I might not have existed & that Thought is more than most can bear.

Perhaps I wander too far. I see I have not made Record of my last visit to the Town after I departed the Forest & before I found my way to this Place. It was upon receiving message from my Mary who said she was desirous of seeing me. Little did I know what to expect of this Encounter. My Trepidation was great, since she has been married almost these two Years past. I found her to my grief weakly confined to sickbed with the Dread consumption in advanced state & but a short time left upon this earth. She said with pitiable smile that she wished but only to take my hand once more before she Departed, for she had known always my Love was True & Great. There was too little I could say as I took that tiny & Tender hand in mine so wasted already, for it seemed grief would permit words scant passage from my Throat. Yet I told her then, with her sad husband briefly Banished from the room, that I should never Love again if I lived a thousand years & God knows that may be the Truth. This might not have been said to the Good for the poor creature then wept profusely & sobbed loudly such as I have never seen a Woman weep before & it was all I could do to still her sobs with Gentle words and less passionate things said before her Husband made solemn return to the room. Her tears no doubt were for the Happiness which Time & Life had stolen from us but her husband has plainly been a good man & kindly & where then should be her grief and discontent? God help us all. We humans are such Poor Frail things & full of mysteries for which there is no accounting or reckoning unless on the Day of Judgement. Mary my poor Mary took much comfort in the notion that somewhere beyond that Day there would be true meeting of our souls in some other peaceful world where all is Music & Light perpetual. Would that I could see this now as I sweat & grope amid the clay of this grey graveyard of Nature where I have come in the months since that Farewell, & fetch out the nuggets which sometimes seem no less than the broken earthbound souls of forest trees whose proud flesh is long Dust, & I see our existence here may not be that much more. If this be so, perhaps Mary's soul & mine may yet be excavated tediously, by someone I cannot yet guess or imagine, & when Scraped & Cleaned shine out with the mystery of what we were & are. I have heard since that Mary is now beyond all Human reach & hurts & comfort but I did not need to be told this News. It is the Truth then. I shall Truly never have the pain & grief of Love again. So there is Freedom in this great graveyard where I toil. May God forgive lovers all.

Peace, friend. Peace. From that future Pike a century hence. Not respect. Not gratitude. Just the wish. For I find you were here once too.

In late afternoon I proceeded to the sea, to examine what work my net had done. There had been hit after hit. Mullet, taken on the turning tide, were tangling in the mesh, with small explosions along the line of corks. Altogether satisfyingly; I could already taste the sweetly smoky flesh. When the tide sank still more, I began to wade with bag and spear, collecting my catch. Preoccupied enough not to notice the shore. When I looked up, Irene was standing solitary there. She could have been on the beach some time, for all I knew. I waved and called; her return was rather limp and silent. That underlined the odd thing. She was standing still, quite still. Terror, for once, wasn't chasing around her, scrambling after sticks. He stood still too, at her feet, looking up patiently. A slightly forlorn picture, but I hadn't the time to consider it closer. Not with the churning fish, the net to be gathered. It was some time before I got back to the dry. First with the bagged mullet, then with the bundled net. Finally I walked along the rocks to where they waited on the sand.

I said, perhaps too brightly, 'Your ancient fisherman friend may make an offering for the communal table.'

She preferred to say nothing, for a while. Then, 'That's the trouble. I can't. Not this time.' The tone was bleak.

'No?'

'I sneaked out this time. There was no one around, so I sneaked out quick. Before anyone knew.'

'I see.' Said for comfort, not from comprehension. Her face was agitated.

'I'm not supposed to go out at all. Not any more.'

'What's the news then? Brother Daniels running a penal colony now?'

'It was a vote. A collective decision. Everyone voted. I could too, only I didn't. Because it was a vote on me, you see. So I didn't think I should. And I didn't.'

It was still too much to manage. 'So what,' I asked, 'have you done?'

'It's what I haven't. I haven't talked at all, you see.'

'About what?'

'About me. You. Us. Like I promised. I didn't talk at all.'

'Sweet Jesus,' I uttered, the elation of the mullet gone.

'They knew something was up after all. These trips of mine. Someone guessed and followed. And heard Terror barking through the trees, you see. And spied. There we were on the beach. I don't know what they saw. Enough, probably. Enough to make things wild.'

The distress was still more distinct now. And Terror was licking her legs, as if in comfort.

I sat down heavy on the sand. I had to.

'Can't you say something to help?' she asked.

'I can say I'm sorry.'

'That's no help.' She sniffed; I didn't care to observe the watering eyes. Otherwise it might all have been laughable, in a way. I could wish ferociously that it was. And wish that wishing would make it so.

'I didn't mean to spoil your life up there.' Also hoping that might be true. 'If that's the life you want.'

'It is,' she insisted. 'It's all I have.'

It was true she had put that point before. But it had no less pungency put a second time.

'Then I'm even more sorry.'

'It's still no help. What makes things worse is it was you. You on this beach with me.'

'And Terror too. Didn't you explain him?'

'I didn't explain anything. Anyway he doesn't count. You do. The way things are, you're bad news. An enemy. Don't you see?'

'You could plead turning the other cheek. Rather pleasantly too.'

That fell stony; everything did.

'If only you'd apologised to Frank. That might have made it better. Not much, but a little. But you wouldn't.'

'There's been no occasion. Anyway it seems he's busy making friends, not pacifying enemies.'

'Please be practical.'

'I can't see where to begin.' More than true, in that strange landscape, where fancies burgeoned like boulders on the moon.

98

'You could let me break my promise. Let me talk about you, us.'

'The hell with that.' I could say that swiftly enough.

'Does it matter, really?'

'Yes. It matters really.' Though I wouldn't have cared to say why, even if I could.

'They'll throw me out if I don't reconsider and tell it like it was. There'll be another vote, and they'll throw me out. That's what will happen now. What can I do? You tell me.' She slumped in the sand beside me.

I had, of course, insufficient to offer. But I placed an arm around her without large effort. Terror approved; he licked us both impartially. Her head fell forward on my chest with a sharp sob; her thin body shook. I looked seaward to where Foster the fisherman was tethering his boat on the tide and tugging in the last of his nets; and took a big breath.

'It'll be all right,' I tried to say. 'The world's still here. Second hand perhaps, tatty at the edges, frayed here and there, but not worth wasting.' It was a truth I found demonstrable, if not impressive consolation. But the best I could do. My bag of fish and bundled net sat shiny on the rocks in the late sun; there was a pale drift of gulls gathering round; the back-lit sea was serenely silvered. 'Take another look. Go on.'

But it seemed her tears were too blinding; she couldn't look. Instead she sobbed again. 'It's all spoiled. I know that now. Even if I go back. They won't trust me again. Even if they let me stay. Can't you see?'

I tried to, since this was expected, and saw something less than nothing, or worse: deception, illusion, fabrication, hallucination, intricate lies for living. But perhaps in the end no worse than any others. No worse than mine, and just as functional. God help us all. We humans are such Poor Frail things & full of mysteries for which there is no accounting or reckoning unless on the Day of Judgement.

'If that's the case,' I argued mildly, 'then it's conceivable that you might be better off without them altogether.' I tried to be tender.

'But what will happen to me?' she appealed, still heavy and heaving on my chest. She was still a child, just a bloody child; what had I done, what was I doing? That couldn't be left till judgement, unless it had come. But the world of Foster the fisherman, out there, still seemed solid. 'I can't think what will happen.'

Suggest she might merely survive after all? Too vague; too elusive and cruel a concept for her to encounter at an age when life had to have point. Purpose. What, then? I was quite empty of utterance, which wouldn't do at all. But I had my arm around her, and could hold her tighter. That seemed to help; the heaving lessened.

'I can't even think where to go,' she said.

Perhaps I could manage a practical observation. 'You must have friends somewhere,' I argued. 'This office where you worked, for example.'

Thoughtless. The suggestion made her shudder.

'Or your parents,' I went on swiftly. 'What about them?'

Another shudder. 'You don't understand,' she said.

Plainly. I tried silence.

'I walked away from all that,' she added angrily. 'That world. It's all behind. I can't go back. And who'd want me back anyway?'

I was in no position to say: I didn't try.

'I'm on my own, if I leave. If they throw me out. On my own.'

'Which is never as unique as it seems,' I suggested as mildly as I could. But again thoughtlessly, it appeared. Rather than consider the possibility she renewed her tears.

'And besides – ' She choked. 'Besides, I have to be among people like myself, don't I? I have to be. I can't make the scene anywhere else. Not the way I am.'

'What way is that?' Perhaps precision was too much to ask.

'You know. I've told you.'

'Not everything.'

She seemed reluctant. 'It's not important,' she insisted. 'It's where I'm at now that's important. I'm nowhere.'

I might effortlessly have argued that she take account of the soft sand under her backside, and the rocks and sea and trees vivid around. But we seemed to have been there before. Besides, her tears were drying. She stirred within my arm. Her body was a light, fluttery thing. Full of fitful and fearful tremblings. And perhaps a dozen disparate urgencies. Some might be discernible; not all.

'You might try telling me I'm not,' she said softly. 'You might try telling me I'm somewhere again. You could take me the way you did last time, if you like.'

Which put one thing in its place. Was all the rest, then, just preliminary? In effect, perhaps. Not in intention. I couldn't believe that. She was too unnerved, too upset. And out of character up to this point. Even Terror had been ignored, though still sleepily patient for affection beside her.

'We were good together,' she reminded me, and slid a hand under my shirt. 'Don't you want to?'

The idea wasn't without appeal, or hazard; the sun, after all, was starting to stain the west. But the colour was early and cool and my flesh warm with the memory of hers.

Nevertheless I took her shoulders suddenly and held her at a distance, slight and shivering, with those hurt animal eyes. It wasn't a comfortable gesture or meant to be.

'Just one thing,' I said, 'before this goes too far. No tricks, no game?'

'I don't know what you mean. Tricks and games aren't my bag.'

'I shouldn't like to think you were here on Mr. Daniels' behalf after all.'

'How can you say that? He's called me terrible things. You can't think that.'

I could. But no matter. 'Never mind,' I said.

'You don't trust me, do you? Or anyone.'

'Probably not. Even myself, most of the time.'

For I still held her roughly at a distance, if with moistening palms, despite her clear wish otherwise, and perhaps mine too. As if to see what the situation said. But it announced itself only, no more. How could it anyway? Flesh was a fact. Something we were doomed to live within, perhaps for purpose. God knew. And He wasn't telling. It was all our bag.

So I drew her back to me, tight and trembling, and felt her sharp limbs soften under my hands, then soon opening and closing around me, as our separate shapes made singular sense. Perhaps not as stunningly as the first time, but still stunning enough. Her body announced shock after shock of pleasure, her mouth awash with wild words, until I rose enormously to the occasion too, no longer indifferent or free of fever in that confused commitment. The relief was real.

'See?' she said presently. 'It was just as good.'

The sky was vivid too, quite suddenly, with vastly coloured clouds. That needed some explanation.

'We were right the first time,' she insisted. 'It wasn't an accident. We're cool, really cool.'

And the dark was already edging into the estuary, smudging coves and crevices, taking residence under the trees. Foster had long gathered his nets and gone.

'Now what?' she went on. 'I can't go back now.'

I was slower to comprehend. I rose and dressed. 'No,' I agreed finally. 'I expect not.' Terror unfolded himself leanly and gave a hungry whimper, his evening meal late, as he rubbed against my legs.

'Is that all you can say?' she asked.

'Also that it's time to think about eating.'

And my net and mullet, quite forgotten. I went across the rocks to fetch them. I could brine the fish overnight, smoke them in the morning; there was sudden pronounced pleasure in renewing routine and resuming the season. In fair mood, then, I strung the net to dry across nearby branches, and carried the bag back to the beach where Irene and Terror waited. We began to climb the track home.

'Just one thing,' she said. 'It's after sunset.' Perhaps she smiled; it was dim under the trees, difficult to see.

'So I've noticed.'

'Good. I wondered, you see.'

We continued our climb.

'I'll try not to make it matter,' she promised.

I found nothing to say. At the house I dropped the bag of mullet on the step, opened the door, stood aside and allowed her entrance to my evening, and perhaps more. A relief, in a sense, that there was no choice.

Later, with Terror fed, mullet brined, food cooking, we sat with wine. She began, at length, to fidget. Perhaps the unfamiliar house, the unfamiliar music; perhaps other things.

'I won't sleep in your bed,' she announced. 'Not if you don't want me there. If it would make you feel better about having me here.'

I didn't see that as something demanding decision. I let it pass and replaced a record. There was no point in not seeing the *Flute* through, once begun. But I kept the volume modest. And asked, 'You don't mind this?'

'As long as you like it. Your pad, isn't it?' She was nervously insistent on remembering that, and I found the insistence touching. Others bustled into the kitchen, trying to take over, before cut short. There was reason to be grateful, if I wanted reason.

'Try to be comfortable anyway,' I suggested.

'Can I talk about tomorrow?' she asked timidly.

'If you must.'

'I could go, easy enough. I don't know where. But I could.'

'Yes,' I agreed. Perhaps it could be safely left at that. Rather than be pursued at peril.

But she went on, 'I might be able to help you, some way. I don't know how. I'm not much use at housework. I can see you don't need looking after.'

'No.' That answer was quick.

'But perhaps with your work. Your pottery. There might be something I could help with. Packing things or something. Little things to help.'

I was about to stop her short of hope when I recalled, suddenly, my promise to Tom Hyde. Money; cheques from Janet; more pots. I was committed to producing at full stretch, for a time, to make that promise pay; and live too. It stood thinking about. So did some help.

'Let's see how tomorrow turns out,' I said finally.

'You're not really saying anything,' she observed.

'No. Probably not.'

Better to hear what Mozart had to say, if we could. But soon the smell of food became more urgent. I rose and moved towards the kitchen.

'You don't have to agree to anything,' she said. 'I'm in no position to push you, am I? I'm in no position for anything much. You can see that, can't you?'

I could indeed. That was the problem. My seconds, flawed by flame, could be dispersed swiftly with a hammer. Not this one, brutally or otherwise. I couldn't wish it away, or drink it aside. It sat too tangibly on my couch.

'I'm sorry,' she finished. 'I'm just pretending to be practical.'

'Then let's eat. That's practical.'

So, later that evening, was her use of my bed. For one thing, no other bed currently functioned.

Not long before dawn I rose and walked barefoot through the house and the mild summer darkness to this desk where two journals reside. Birds began to flute in the trees outside; the windows lightened; the estuary became visible in a gentle glow. Until I inhabited another tomorrow. It is the Truth then. I shall truly never have the pain & grief of Love again. But Freedom, old friend? Never.

Yet it should be easy enough soon to find my bed again, and share it usefully with a stranger.

7

November 27:

SUMMER AGAIN. AND TRUE SUMMER, IT SEEMS, A MONTH SHORT of the longest day. Thick heat. Manuka and kanuka flower, frosting those mostly drab trees, and dry clay cracking underfoot, already hugely fissured in places despite the recent rain. The flotsam weed gathers still thicker on the beach, with my compost taking its flavour. Early morning is best for work, before the heat grips, with cool clear light, hills without haze, and the estuary brittle with beauty. For work appears imperative now. Irene and I make most use of the morning; afternoons and evenings are left to look after themselves. Another firing has begun. The mullet emerged from the smokehouse tender and sweet; Rose and Tony pronounce them my best ever, and they bring some seasonal piquance to our table. Things could have been less pleasant.

Much less. For Daniels arrived, of course, two or three days after Irene's departure from his establishment. Terror's barking gave first signal while we took coffee break in the house at mid-morning. Then Irene observed his approach from the window, and fled to the bedroom. I met him at the door, and didn't invite him in.

'Sorry about this,' he began.

'So am I,' I said. 'I'm working.'

And walked past him, down towards the wheel under the lean-to. He followed slow.

'It's about a member of our community,' he went on. 'A girl. She's left suddenly. We're not sure where. But we've reason to believe you might know.'

'Oh?'

'She was seen once with you. We feel she might have turned up here.'

We arrived at the lean-to. I began to work some clay. 'Feel what you like,' I offered. 'No skin off my nose.'

Perhaps not the fashionable phrase. He seemed perplexed. 'It's just we feel you should be warned.'

'Warned, or threatened?'

'Please don't misunderstand. A friendly warning. About the girl herself. Nothing aimed at you. Advice, if anything. Perhaps I've put it poorly.'

'Try again,' I suggested. The clay was stiff, but beginning to give.

'She's a most unstable personality. Confused. A compulsive liar and fantasist.'

'So what's the message?'

'You'd be taking a risk if you have her here. She could be dangerous. We've done our best. There've been some bad scenes. But we'd like to think the community situation, the constraint of collective living, has done her some good. Now this. We hate to think what might happen. Not just to her. To anyone getting involved. It's on our conscience.'

'Admirable,' I observed. The clay was telling me to get on with it.

'Especially,' he added, 'if things turn out badly. We'd feel responsible, in a sense. You must see that.'

'In a sense,' I agreed. 'I find I can see most things in a sense. If pressed, that is. And you seem to be pressing me now.'

'I'm sorry to break in on your work. But I felt the importance of the thing justified the urgency, if you take my meaning.'

'I'll try.'

'I'm only trying to tune you in as best I can.'

'And I'm telling you to fuck off as best I can.' For the clay couldn't wait now. Nor could I. Daniels disappeared.

'It's all right now?' Irene asked anxiously.

'Yes,' I answered. 'And if it isn't, we shall pretend it is.'

Thereafter a good morning for work, with shelves filling fast. Nothing like adrenalin as additive to speed the clay.

Terror stalked around us, back and forward, and finally curled calm near our feet. In the afternoon we took him down through the trees to the sea, where he pissed profusely in promising places, and scurried after the sticks we threw. Until he tired to a trot, quit altogether, and slept in shade. We pursued our own pleasure on the sand.

'I don't have to pretend anything,' she said. 'I know it's all right. I'm safe.'

That night, though, she woke with sweats. Small cries of alarm. I groped blearily for the bedside lamp, switched it on and asked, 'What's wrong?'

She was blinded; she covered her eyes. 'Nothing,' she said. Then, 'It's just I'm afraid again.'

'What of? Daniels?' I became more lucid with the light. 'Forget him. Consider that he might even be more afraid than you are; I had that impression.'

'Not just him. Everything.' She started to shiver.

I tried to calm her in familiar fashion. But it was plainly

inadequate to the moment. 'All right,' I said. 'So tell me about everything.'

She shook her head. 'When it's like this, it's too much to tell. It's just everything, that's all. Everything.'

'So take it slowly.'

'I'm dying.' This emerged as a savage cry. 'Can't you understand?'

It seemed I might have to try.

'And switch off that light. It's cruel.'

So was the prospect of another cry like that. The light went off. Not that the dark diminished her disturbance. For she said as shrilly, 'Get me something. Quick.'

'Something? What?'

'Something to knock me out quick. Before it gets worse. You must have something.'

I had to think, if possible. I staggered out of the bedroom, through the dark house, suffering only minor collision with the couch on my way; and arrived in the bathroom. In the medicine cabinet, searching diverse debris of a painful past, I groped among clinking containers and found a half-forgotten bottle of barbiturates. They might serve as something. I padded back to the bedroom. 'Here,' I said. 'Try these.'

'What are they?'

I told her, roughly.

'Is that all?'

'They're strong, as I recall. One should do the trick.'

'One?' she said. 'You have to be joking. Get me something to wash them down. Some of that wine. A big glass. Big as you can make it.'

'That's not a healthy mix,' I protested.

'Well, I'm not healthy either. Quick.'

So I fetched a tumbler of red nevertheless. And journeyed back to her side, switching on the light again while passing over the wine. She shook a pile of pills in her palm and, before I could say anything, flipped most into her mouth.

'For God's sake,' I shouted. I swung a hand and sent the bottle spinning; pills rattled across the bedroom floor. The wine spilled too.

'Why?' she said. 'Why did you do that?' And swallowed fast.

'All those. You're out of your mind.'

'Right on,' she agreed. 'That's why I need them.'

'And that wine too.'

'That'll just help them swing. They don't amount to much, those things. Kid stuff.'

She was suddenly a hard little hippie again, with acid tone. Telling a poor square like it is. Kid stuff? I could tell her tales. But there was hardly a hope. I was sweating fast, and trembling too.

'All right,' I said, slow to calm. 'But just don't give me another fright like that.'

'What the hell. It's me who's got the frighteners on. Can't you see?'

I could; no sweat. But she soon grew soft, and pleasantly hazy. Finally she extended her arms. 'Here,' she said. 'Here, lover man.' Dreamily on the pillow.

I might have preferred more choice. But anything to help us through the night. Not that it mattered. For the act amounted in the end to no more than necrophilia. It left me sharply awoken while she slept. I tried to persuade my frigid frame that peace was still possible that night. No use. So I quit my business with the dark, rose and dressed, and considered less troubling transactions. This took me through the house, with Terror tramping behind, and at last to this desk; and two journals asking attention. With no hesitation I chose the older of the pair; it might invite less answer. Though that was no huge hope, the way things were. That future Pike a century hence still had to answer for himself, in the end.

April 16, 1875: Today I felt upon my face, whilst I worked outdoors, the first pure fresh wind of Winter. Perhaps Frost is not too long away. Thus tonight I have built my fire large against the advance of Cold, after cooking my meal, & by fire-light & candlelight sit here Pen in Hand to contemplate what this long dying Summer has seen. For try as I might I cannot recall a longer Summer nor a Harder one in all my Years which now begin to seem many & more than I care to count upon this Earth & in this New Land which after all now begins to seem mine for all its strangeness & where New Life seems in truth begun. For I now walk acres I can call my own & if that is no great Triumph there is still comfort in the Truth that none can say otherwise & by that I mean no mere Mortal man. How the Dead might regard me, those brown men who in-habited this Land before, is a matter of no great moment or concern to me, & I cannot imagine even God feeling too posses-sive about this place, if He ever has pause in his many affairs to look this way. But I begin to wander in this Evening glow, perhaps persuaded so by Visions leaping upon the flames of my Fire which is all I have between myself & the dark & silences beyond this dwelling I have lately built for my shelter among these Lonely Hills. This warmth is of my own making & I can Say the same fairly of this Summer too. The asking price of this Land was cheap enough & within my means when I En-countered it a year or less ago, for all that it seems another Lifetime. It was once Maorie holding for all that matters & then bought & sold with larger estate & then finally a scrap fallen from a more fertile Table. Nonetheless to be devoured hungrily by me, when first I sighted it & saw some Possibility in the place which none had risked in the race for Easier Profit. The timber here is too scrappy & scattered to make for much & the rest mostly scrubby stuff & the gumland of whitish clay well worked over by dozens of diggers in the recent Past. All the Past is recent here if one but only thinks. The Past is no cold dead thing but a live warm thing of men still Living & Breathing & walking, hardly to be called so at all, unless of course one again thinks of those others of different Complexion in earlier Time. There has been but one Occasion here to think thus, a burial cave I discovered in a cave in an outlying part of this Property, bones mostly, skulls & scraps of rotted garments here & there & a few trinkets & adornments worked from green Jade of sorts found in these islands which I thought might be of some Value. I collected them & brought them into my dwelling, thinking to dispose of them profitably in Town on some Future occasion. That night the timber creaked around me & I slept ill & recalled tales of old Maorie curses. Next day I returned these things where they properly belonged & altogether think them well left alone for my peace of mind & also the location of that cave too is best forgotten if I hope to be free of all taint from that dead Past & live clean in the Present as if none had been before me. This I can at Times well believe as I launch myself upon the task of taming this Land.

The Summer has been all a thing of Fire & I mean not merely the hot sun sometimes hovering savage in the sky above me while I toil. When I had won what timber I wanted for this dwelling & for future purpose such as fences & the like I then made it my business to put it to the torch. The conflagrations resulting were sometimes a spectacle beyond all imagining, even if all my making, with flame licking tall up the trees & roaring through the lesser growth & smoke pouring down the hillsides upon the wind & at other times great columns towering dark upon the Horizon as if announcing my presence here & that Man had come at last & was Master. It was no small thing of a Day but week after week once begun with fire sometimes sputtering down or dampened altogether in Summer rain which could be setback when Heavy. Now the task is mostly Done, with axe & saw & flame. The ash is thick upon the hillsides & will nourish the grass seed I scatter. With spring this Land will grow green again & soon with fences built & livestock wandering & grazing the pastures & there will be something not unlike an Eden made in this wilderness place, my homestead amid gardens & English trees & perhaps thrushes warbling & blackbirds singing & wisps of smoke from that sturdy chimney above & the name Pike planted & rooted secure in this Land. For already I can see end here to my journeys & griefs of the past & Life Anew. Perhaps the flames of my Fire again persuade me to Visions. Man cannot live long without Such. I remember my Austrian friend upon the Gumfields & his talk on long Evenings while we cleaned & scraped. The Memory has sadness, for the Truth is his Wife died of some ill before he could Finance her voyage to join him here & ere long he took to the Drink in despair.

I should be thinking rather of the tasks of Winter now soon upon me, such as extending this dwelling with the Timbers set aside for the purpose & making it more habitable for the life & lives to come. For I cannot doubt that there is more life than one & more than merely my span in Contention here. I must give some thought also to removing the stumps of the larger trees which remain rooted in this property, first those about the dwelling & then those in wider & wider circle around while pasture grows & this may have no end in my lifetime once begun. Yet I cherish the thought of beginning a task now which my Grandson might finish while he perhaps considers my winning of this Wilderness for the name Pike & shares in the last of it. Again it seems Vision bears me away, before this Fire, as if upon Wild Chariot. I may while the moment lasts permit myself one Impossible Dream or wish which is no less than that I would Mary my poor lost Mary were with me now sharing this domain, to see my acres grow green around & all things flower as if in Man's first spring. I can scarce bring myself to Set this Down in words, this sad Lunatic wish, for I find a lump of pain which is still not numb enough & far too tender at the edge & thus best left alone if I can will it. For Mary if I but dare think is now no more than those poor bones & rotted garments I found in that old Maorie

113

burial cave & thought of her is likewise best well left alone for my peace of mind & if I hope to be free of all taints from the Past & live clean in the Present not so much for my own sake as for the Future's. It seems sleep has at last begun to undo me while I set this down, so perhaps a little Honesty is a useful thing at times & may rid me of wilder Dreams & longings. I shall remove my tired & sore limbs from before this fire & retire to my bachelor bed & embrace precious Sleep as my mistress while the fire burns low.

I wished to hell sleep would undo or embrace me, as mistress, assassin, anything, technically a matter of indifference. But too soon there was a glimmer of grey on the estuary; and a bubbling pot of coffee to begin my day briskly. While he slept dreamless. He earned it, at least. My own fire could hardly have burned lower. So I travelled through the coffee to the clay. A little Honesty is a useful thing at times & may rid me of wilder Dreams & longings.

Irene, surprisingly, joined me under the lean-to later that morning. Not too much later, either. She had fresh coffee and a shaky smile.

We didn't discuss the night until some time into the afternoon, with pressure eased. Then vaguely, at first.

'I'm sorry,' she said, 'if I gave you a fright.'

'It's all right,' I answered. And wished that the truth.

'I hope it doesn't happen again.'

'We'll make that mutual.'

We were on the beach. The sun high. The tide risen. Trees fresh with shiny leaf. And Terror, run ragged after sticks, now asleep on the sunny sand. It was hard to recall the night as real.

'It might help,' she continued, 'if you got me something better. Stronger. Just in case.'

'Better?' I said. 'Stronger?' I was slow to understand.

'Pills,' she explained, and named the most desirable kind. A name unfamiliar to me, but that was irrelevant. 'Your doctor would prescribe them, if you asked. If you said you had a problem. You're trustworthy. He's allowed to prescribe them. Quite simple.'

'Perhaps,' I said. Then suddenly, 'The hell with it, though, until I know what's going on. And what has been. It's time for truth.'

She looked hurt. That was no feat. I had seldom seen her as looking less than bruised, and braced for worse. However much I might prefer to see her otherwise.

'Come on,' I said.

'I've told you most things.'

'Not everything.'

'No,' she admitted. Shy again. She looked down at the sand intensely, as if trying to focus on separate grains.

'Well?'

'It's difficult to explain.'

'I imagine it is. I'll make allowances.'

'You won't make trouble, will you?'

'For who?'

'Me. Anyone. You could, you see.'

'All right. I won't rock boats.'

'I want a promise you'll keep. I kept mine. You keep yours.'

'I'll try.'

'All right,' she said, and took deep breath.

It was hardly illumination she offered in the end. Not then, not there. For it was all too slight in substance beside her forlorn presence on the beach. What I didn't know already I could possibly have proposed to myself anyway, as working hypothesis. Her incoherent intimations and casual confessions, fragments, phrases, were an easy harvest. Then the picture was precise. A girl prey to despair, possibly real enough, pops a few pills and gives herself fearful fright. Needing help, she is easily persuaded she is a junkie or the next best thing; and soon enough she is the next best thing. For cold turkey can be painful, as even the uninitiated know, as newspapers and magazines often tell, and so the way back becomes a prospect of pills and powders, and yet more pills and powders, in some considered measure, to keep panic clear. While love, or talk of it, bathes all in blissful glow; and the sharing and caring or what passes for same soon seems best and most earnestly expressed in sexual terms. With friend Daniels, doubtless, king of the fowlyard; but I interpolate unfairly. Her fits and starts made progression slow towards that point. And finally anyway – again it seems I cannot resist the interpolation – it seemed to me an elaborate and unnecessarily tortuous way of arriving at a good old-fashioned gang bang, albeit long running with changes of venue.

If that was truth, it was distinctly something I could have done without. And with no real deprivation. As things were, I felt dimly dirtied. What would that older Pike, stolid on his fiery frontier, have made of such a tale? Better the first pure fresh wind of Winter, old friend. This is the tawdry growth your ash and sweat has nourished. For the first time I envied him his century.

So we sat in silence, with Terror deeply dozing.

'You don't say much,' she announced at last.

'No,' I agreed.

'Is it so terrible?'

'Sad. Mostly.'

'I've upset you.'

'I take a lot of upsetting. That's the general feeling.'

'I'm sorry if I have.'

'I asked for truth. I can't complain.'

'You can't think much of me now. You must think I'm weak.'

'No one lives long enough to be strong. It's all been badly arranged.'

'Anyway I have been. But I'm getting stronger. Here, with

116

you and Terror. Except for last night, and I'm sorry about that, I really am. Really. Truly.' All said quickly, childishly. Next thing she might cross her heart and hope to die before she told a lie. That earnest innocent could make me flinch as much as the hard little hippie in my bed.

'It's all right,' I insisted.

'But you can't really think much of me.'

'Often I don't think at all. In that sense. The sense of passing judgement. I lost my licence.'

'And I suppose you mightn't even want to touch me again.'

She had a point there of sorts. But not one I could consider with comfort. So I didn't.

'Better,' I suggested, 'if we didn't talk of pills again. Pills and magic potions on prescription.'

That left her downcast briefly. But soon she lifted her head and experimented with a smile.

'Then,' I went on, 'you might see whether you have half a chance of living your life without prescription. From Doctor Daniels or anyone else.'

'The thing is, nothing seemed so very wrong at the time.'

'No. I expect not.'

'What people wanted to do with themselves seemed to be their own business.'

'It arguably is, most of the time.'

'Do you really believe that?'

'With difficulty. And long qualifications, like the fine print in an insurance policy, down below.'

'I see,' she said, even if she didn't. For she still appeared, after all, to desire judgement passed. She wanted right and wrong in bold type, not down there in the fine print. That would be comfort, God knew; less strain on the vision for us all. 'It was only at the end, when I fell out with the others, that I really saw something wrong. Sick wrong, I mean. I couldn't tell what it was exactly. I just saw it.'

'When they took away the pills and potions?'

'Even pot. They wouldn't even pass the pot to me in the evenings. Until I talked. I didn't know I could be that strong. But I was.'

'So there's a start.'

'I didn't know why I was strong either. Except that I was mad at their meanness. But I think I do now. I think I know why I was strong now.'

'Oh?' Another start, perhaps.

'I think it was because I was beginning to be in love with you.'

She hadn't seen me angry before, and looked stunned when I shouted. 'We are not,' I told her, 'going to talk about drugs. Not any more.'

Even Terror leapt out of sleep at so vehement a voice. Then he trailed us home, possibly baffled by the silence which followed.

Evening was easier at first. No more than a fidget or two in passing, and she would likely have preferred something livelier from my record player. But still, for the most part pleasant; she again tried patiently to share what I heard in a man called Mozart. Since I professed to hear most things, given average human hearing. Even, at the end, the fire and water. She seemed to suffer no large chill; perhaps the warmth of the wine with which I plied her. She was drowsy enough by the time she pleaded need for bed, which was more or less my intention. She was soon asleep. I walked through the soundless house, found a pipe as comfort, and a deep chair. But soon the wine told on me too; I drifted about the edge of sleep.

Her cry, though, tugged me back from that tide. This time I was ready, and sprinted to the bed. She was wild again, trembling with need, one large flurry of fright.

'Those pills again,' she called, though I was close.

'Not this time,' I said. 'Too easy.'

'You bastard.'

'Yes,' I agreed. 'Altogether.'

I held down her sweaty limbs for a time. Then I fetched hot water, and a cloth, and tried to bathe her back into the world. Like a child. Like birth, or christening.

Then black coffee.

'It's just I get scared,' she confessed, when she ceased to shake. 'It's not that I'm really so hooked on anything.'

'No,' I said. 'I can see that.'

'So long as you don't mind me being a bit hooked on you.'

'It shouldn't be essential.'

'Yes. It is. Please.'

Certainly she was clean enough now. But I took her more lightly than before, as if afraid of bruise or fracture. There could be no end to the damage done.

8

December 6:

MY ENTRIES BEGIN TO THIN WITH THE SUMMER, AND OTHER things. Other things? The wheel; the kiln. The smoke from our frequent firings makes almost permanent blue mist among the trees. And if not from the kiln, then from the smokehouse; the mullet are running heavy now. Wild waves, in sudden storm last week, gouged the last of the weed from the beach; the sand is clean and white again when we walk there. The old pohutu-kawa along the shore are pale with tender leaves and buds, freshening for the scarlet bloom of Christmas. My garden, still a place of strong aroma, composted from land and sea, is about to produce. Capsicum and cucumber should arrive well before year's end, with beans and tomatoes following soon. I keep the bugs at bay.

Irene? Yes, to be fair. To make full account, that is. She has improved, one might say, out of sight. But one might also not, even if one wished to resurrect the awkward old square usage of the phrase, since she insists on occupation of much of my day, seldom further out of sight than middle distance. And wholly in close up in awakenings.

Since she wished to make herself seem useful, she tried the kitchen, with disasters. So I have preferred to keep her closer to the clay. Her glazing is proficient, and she has offered ideas of her own. That is, fetching and carrying aside; and mugs of coffee. And today, seeing no reason why not, I actually persuaded her to the wheel, to see what happened. I sat to one side and lit my pipe.

What happened, though not really remarkable, was that I saw I might have to take her more seriously. She was nervous at the wheel, rather desperately containing the clay as it turned. Then, as confidence came, as I urged her on, it became plain that she had been watching more closely than I thought, taking in my technique, even the bolder gestures along with the smaller, the slapdash indifference one can contrive as cover for caring.

'You don't have to do exactly as I do,' I explained at length. 'Find your own feel. Your own style.'

She looked dismayed. 'What's that?'

'What we are, individually.'

'But what am I?'

Her problem. Now mine too, it seemed.

'God knows. But try and find out.'

'But what if I'm not much? How can I make anything much?'

Pathetic. But I declined to be moved. That way ran risk. I argued her back to the wheel. And some fresh clay.

'It's all a game,' I insisted, when her fingers faltered again. And kept on talking, since it seemed to help. 'Perhaps a game with truth. To see if we can make something honest, out of honest substance. It won't be perfect. Honesty never is without flaw. Our kind of honesty, I mean, the human kind. Because it never amounts to more than the best we can do, and that's never enough. So it's just a game, a gamble. Like everything else; anything we do. Don't try to be me, because that's a lie. You're a different and utterly unique arrangement of skin and nerve and bone. So see what your own hands say about it all. And that clay. Come on. Take the gamble. Play the game.'

This worked, up to a point. After perhaps an hour she had something which might lumpily pass for a pot.

'There,' I said. 'You can glaze that. And put it through the fire. Your own thing. How does that grab you?'

Not too strongly, it appeared. For she was still bent over her tiny triumph. Weak with relief, no doubt.

I put my pipe aside, stood up, and took her by the shoulders. And turned her around, face upwards. Then I had my answer, saw just how it had grabbed her. She had been weeping on the wheel.

'It's not a game, is it?' she asked in small voice later this morning, while I worked. 'Not really, is it?'

'Only when it helps to think so,' I confessed.

'What does that mean?'

'When it isn't, nothing is. Nothing's a game.'

That left her quiet. Perhaps my tone. And at that point, for some reason, the rising clay crumpled under my hands.

'Come on,' I said, wiping myself off. 'We can call it quits for now.'

She was grateful to agree. Difficult to see it as an experiment to repeat too soon. But I know we shall.

Tom Hyde called. 'Thanks for the cheque,' he said. 'I know how much it means to you.'

'It means five hundred and twelve dollars fifty.'

'All the same –'

'There should be another on the way soon.'

'Well, it means a lot to us anyway. Cash to fight with. We'll soon have the bastards on the run and the estuary safe.'

'So just bring me the good news then.'

'It looks as if you have some already.' He eyed Irene under the lean-to with knowing smile. 'You got assistance now?'

'Now I'm in full production, yes. I need it.' I wasn't going to give him satisfaction. 'She's useful.'

'So I see.'

Daniels hasn't called again. But I don't doubt he knows by now that Irene is here. The ferns of Rangiwai make no great green wall beyond which she can hide forever. They may simply serve to frame a pleasantly peacfeul picture, or an unpleasantly potent one, depending on the eyes of the beholder. And I never much cared for Daniels' eyes in any case.

But the point, if point there must be, is that he doesn't come, or try to contact Irene discreetly. His own stolen chicken. He may, of course, be trying to repair the netting after her flight. Possibly he is paralytic with fear; I should like to think so. And waiting for the police to call. In which case the paralysis will be slow to pass, since they are not coming; at least not at my instigation. I hope the bastard roasts, rather slowly.

Janet next. Her van backing down the drive. 'For God's sake,' she said, 'what's going on? A few weeks ago I had to get down on my knees to plead for pots. Now you're threatening to be a glut on the market. What is it?'

'Various things,' I said vaguely. 'I need money.'

'Now you're talking again. But what for? Not maintenance, surely. You said Anna never pressed you.'

'Not maintenance. Not that kind.' For maintenance, after all, might mean more than money. 'I'm just trying to keep myself in reasonable repair.'

'Well,' she went on, 'I should tell you I'm suffering some embarrassment at the moment. One of my selling points with your pots is that the bloody things are scarce, to be bought while the going's good. Now you're making a liar out of me.

You're swamping the shop. The only good thing about it is the season. They're still selling almost as soon as they arrive. But if you keep this up, I won't have room for anything else but Pike.'

'It won't go on forever,' I promised.

'I just want to know why the change, what's happened here to my precious Pike.'

We walked past the house, and flowering garden.

'Come on,' she said. 'Tell all.' Then, from a distance, she saw Irene among my pots. 'And who, may I ask, is she?'

'Assistance mainly. Time I had some.'

'Agreed. But her?'

'Just a kid who turned up here one day. She's made herself useful since.'

'She actually lives here?' asked Janet with wonder.

'For the time being. Yes.'

'That scrap. That little hippie. You've always picked and chosen, Pike. What's happened to you?'

We approached the lean-to then. Janet was polite, Irene on edge. Some amiable conversation passed, mostly business. Then I took Janet up to the house while Irene remained behind.

'Well,' said Janet, taking her glass, 'all else in my day seems to pale. I need a little time to swallow it down. Her, I mean. Not the wine. You were saying?'

'I was saying I'd appreciate your speeding up payment, if you could.'

She evidently found it hard to concentrate. 'All right,' she agreed. 'No problem. If you had to have someone here after all, couldn't you have done better for yourself?'

'In what way?'

'Please, Paul. She can hardly scratch two words together. What can you have in common?'

'Need.'

'Need?'

'Unspecific. Of a season.'

'It gets worse. What about her?'

'She's all right here.'

'Just be careful, Paul. She knows she's on to a good thing. Also I read more into those sheep's eyes. That she thinks she's in love, for example. Just don't get fouled up on her account. It wouldn't be worth it this time.'

'You mean Anna was worth it?'

'Probably, yes. She was, wasn't she?'

A lengthy pause. A stroll through the gallery. Then Anna; and sweet Charlie too.

'All right,' I said, recoiling. 'Just don't go on.'

'Sorry to push. It's just that she's been on my mind. I saw her again the other day.'

'Oh?' A cool touch of winter in the summer heat; a very local frost.

'In the shop again. This time, interestingly, she was openly in search of something of yours. No vagueness at all, no evasion. Just picking her way along the shelf, lingering here and there. She even bought something in the end. One of those large wine jars.'

'You don't remember which one?'

'Not specially; no. Does it matter?'

'Yes,' I said. 'No.'

'Make up your mind.'

'No, then. I'd sooner not know.'

'Poor Paul. Poor Anna too.'

'If you don't mind – '

'But I do mind. I do care. A friend should. And care about what you're both doing with yourselves.'

'Let's keep to business. My side of it, not yours. Who the hell you sell pots to is no concern of mine. Or who the hell you have in your shop.'

'True. I foolishly imagined you might be interested.'

'And you foolishly might be right. So let's leave it.'

'You don't want to hear any more?'

I hesitated, sighed. 'All right. Go on.'

'There isn't much more really. We talked a bit. But you have to remember I never knew Anna well – only casually, in company, at your old house. It's hard to be personal. Aside from public things. But she knows I see you, which makes a difference. And she actually asked after you this time.'

'I see.' Then, 'What did she say?'

'She just asked were you all right. And I told her yes, you were all right. And she said good, that was good. Subject exhausted, you see. So don't agitate yourself. Nothing to it, really.'

'Good.'

'Aside from which, we talked of those public things. This opera. Her singing. It seems she enjoys working towards something again. And her voice, some think, hasn't gone back. There may even be a gain or two.'

'What am I supposed to say?' Though it was more relevant to ask myself how I was supposed to feel. Because I couldn't feel.

'You're not obliged to say anything at all.'

'Good.'

'Anna's all right. That's all you need to know. And you're all right mostly too. That's all she needs to know. I didn't ask to be bearer of tidings. Why don't you make a point of seeing her soon? It wouldn't hurt, surely.'

'You're joking.'

'Never. At this point it might mean a lot to her. And any pain on your side might be worth it, in the end. Besides, you worry me now. When I see what's going on here.'

'My pots aren't falling to pieces?'

'To the best of my knowledge, no.'

'Then I'm not either.'

'Please be careful, Paul. Please. You're not up to it.'

She placed a hand on mine. Warm enough, and well inten-

tioned. Then we went outside and carefully packed the back
of the van with the fragile produce of the Pike acres.

Irene, with evening, and after much apparent thought: 'That
woman today. Who was she?'

'I introduced you, for God's sake. Janet; Janet Harris. She
runs a shop.'

'I mean, who is she really?'

'A friend. An oldish acquaintance. Take your pick.'

'I didn't like her much.'

'Janet has a brusque manner. It can deceive.'

'It wasn't that. It was the way she looked at me. As if I was
nothing. That's all I'll ever be to your friends. Nothing.'

'I'm not exactly surrounded by friends. As you might have
observed.'

'They're probably right anyway. I suppose I am nothing.
Pretty, but not pretty enough. Not clever enough. Not anything
enough, if I think about it.'

'So don't think about it.'

'I have to, don't you see? I can't help it when I'm with you.
Other people can do things. Run shops. Sing. Make beautiful
things. I'm not good for anything.'

Perhaps I should have known better than to pit her against
the clay and the wheel. Given this consequence. For she began
to weep rather desperately. I walked across the room and
grabbed her tight by the shoulders. 'Come on,' I said. 'This
can't do you any good.'

'You were talking about honesty today. As if it was a good
thing.'

'In reasonable measure, yes.'

'I'm just trying to squeeze some out until it hurts.'

'I was talking about an attitude of approach to the clay.
Talking figuratively, not literally.'

'I can't talk that way, whatever it is. I can only say what
I mean.'

127

'So there's an edge you've got on the rest of us.'

I then offered other consolations. Grilled cheese and tomato on toast. Coffee. Some medicinal Irish mist. And finally bed.

Though there seemed some suffering there too. 'That woman Janet,' she said. 'You've slept with her, haven't you?'

'Yes,' I agreed presently. 'Now and then.'

'Was she any good? Tell me.'

'Is it necessary?'

'I think so. Yes.'

'No big thing. Janet's not jealous. You've no cause either.'

'That wasn't what I was asking. I asked was she any good.'

'Adequate,' I answered.

'And what about me? Is that all I am too?'

Her thighs ceased to move under mine.

'I didn't say that.'

'But I need to know, just the same.'

'There's nothing wrong with being adequate,' I insisted. 'It's my entire ambition.'

She had to think about that, evidently. Meanwhile her thighs began moving with me again, rather furtively, as if against her will; and her arms grew tighter around my neck. So I proceeded with the business of proving adequacy, of sorts.

Because it ended well, as always. This time, though, the effort left me sleepless. Afterwards, after all, there was Anna. I could blame Janet's visit. Or myself, with relevance. Adequacy? A poor joke. I was still no more adequate to thought of Anna than I was to her in the flesh, as my cringing consciousness tended to testify. Irene soon slid into sleep. Finally a huge flutter of fright, as if from something uncaged in my body, suggested need beyond bed. After lifting Irene's limp limbs aside, quite carefully, I went through the house to find familiar refuge. His. Mine.

March 4, 1879: Yesterday married Florence Martin after courtship of 1 year and brought her home with me.

128

October 17, 1879: As the years run giddily past, this Journal begins to seem less a Chronicle of my days than an album within which I affix Landmarks in my Life & is perhaps not much the worse for being this. I cannot imagine these pages offering more than dust & boredom to those whose eyes may chance here in that Future still vexingly impossible to discern. What, they might well ask with justice, of that Happy Event inscribed above? Has this man, or Ancestor, no more to say of Himself or indeed of his Bride? Is his Cup of Happiness so full that he could not spare himself a Sidelong Thought? The truth is that this Journal since the entry above has long been out of sight & thus also out of Mind. There are things in these pages which are better left unseen by Florence & which could make for Misunderstandings between us. They rest under a dry floorboard & wrapped in good tough Canvas to keep the rats from nibbling away my Past & leaving me altogether naked. This long & restless night made it seem desirable for me to take it out again & give it some attention & repair as Record. The house is quiet & Florence sleeps the sound sleep of the just. She fast grows large with child & with fortune smiling I may soon have a Son to share my days & one day my Tasks. I cannot deny her credit as Wife for she is good Woman in most respects & if her tongue is inclined sometimes to the Sharper Side the fault perhaps is not always her own since her family the Martins in the next valley are a tribe of sharp tongues & bitter Quarrels & she sometimes I must confess has cause for great impatience with me & what she calls my lunatic dreams of what this Land & the name Pike yet may be. Life, she says, is a Business Proposition & she can quote the Gospel surprisingly in support of such contention when she wishes to make impression on me. There is no place for Dreams in a Business Proposition. They make for no Credit & Pay no interest. I now take her meaning & keep Visions to myself when I walk my acres & sit Lonely before the fire at late hours. They may bring no Interest but they can still be balm to the Flesh as it ages. The green growth of my pastures makes brave bold show this warm & sunny spring & birds sing & all seems serene as Florence fattens. None could recognise this place, this grassy valley with animals wandering & this growing homestead with trees growing shady, as the rough & rugged land I took a few short years ago. Elsewhere such taming of wilderness has been a thing of centuries. Here men make each month of labour count as Decade, as I have. It is all a thing of sweat & Blood & dreams too like mine multiplied thousandsfold. Hush. I find myself listening hard in the dark & Silence lest Florence awaken & hear this heresy. Yet to set this down even if in such furtive fashion helps heal the ache of the Flesh & the wounds of the Spirit & helps a man find Peace when night tells him his Life after all is nothing much. Florence is not my Mary & never will be & it would be unfair to expect other. She will bear Flesh of my Flesh & a man will know all is not for nothing. I can hear wind rise in the trees & the rattle of rain on the roof. I think I can dress these pages in Canvas Shroud & return them to their grave beneath the floorboard & find sleep beside Florence again as the night marches on towards morning & the rest of my Life.

It seemed after all his ambition was no more than adequacy too. I hope he slept well that night. And for the rest of his Life. Unreasonable, then, to feel he fails me now. He was merely a man of his time, as historians have it; and I shall be merely a man of mine, a century hence, should someone ever shovel up the shards left on this land, my shattered and scattered pots, and consider them as cultural curiosity. Or trendy heresy.

9

December 19:

THE RUSH IS OVER. THE LAST WISP OF SMOKE FROM THE KILN
has curled among the trees. And the selling season is over
soon. Janet has sent a telegram, crying mercy; her shelves are
full, with more to come. Tom Hyde has still another cheque to
keep him content. This morning I harvested the first two
capsicums, small and sweet, and sliced our first cucumber for
lunch. Flounder now fill my net, when I peg it out near the
mangrove patch; we breakfast handsomely, Rose and Tony
too. And premature pohutukawa bloom along the shore; the
bees are noisy among the nectar. While we soak up sun upon
the sand, or wade into the tide. The antipodean sloth of the
season has begun to colour our days, just a shade short of
Christmas.

Irene? She has sometimes, lately, been quite out of sight.
Especially when she works upon the wheel. I tell her that
such careful work must make it on the market soon. She
laughs, but wants to believe it. The truth is that I do see some

growing grace in what she does with clay; I may not leave her empty-handed after all.

Beth announces her arrival sometime through the Christmas holidays. A slight blight there, if I allow myself to think about it. I try not to. She shall come if she must. And I imagine she must.

Daniels? Who is he? Perhaps the communal enterprise has foundered beyond the fern. But I still hear now and then, when I walk Terror late in the evening, the faint sounds of hot rock rolling across the ridges and rooftops of Rangiwai.

I propose searching for scallops for Christmas dinner, if low tides are low enough. There is just a thin sprinkle left at the edge of the estuary, a tiny bed or two I try to keep secret, where those shapely shells may be found like lost jewels in the mud. Irene expresses pleasure at the prospect of such a search, then so fine a feast. A cool idea. Really neat.

I stock up on wine, anyway, to see us through. Through to where, though? Precisely, then, through Christmas into yet another year. I haven't the patience for imprecision. Nor had he, when I found him again.

January 2, 1880: My son Joshua John, so christened in emergency, perished this p.m. after life Span of just 48 hours. His lungs, they said, could not properly take the air. Otherwise perfect boy. Florence well.

March 18, 1881: Male child stillborn this p.m. Florence well.

July 7, 1882: Florence announced this a.m. a miscarriage proceeding. Rode to fetch her mother & sister who are now in attendance. Sex of child unknown. Florence recovering.

December 7, 1883: Male child stillborn.

November 16, 1884: Female child born healthy. Florence well.

Enough. More than enough. Of this one too. I find my talent for discourse dead in his unnatural absence; I shall return both journals to their present place of safety, not under a floorboard, but within a crevice behind the couch. Irene has begun to express too great an interest in what I am composing here. She does not believe I am merely keeping accounts, which is my devious explanation. Yet the truth.

10

January 4:

FIRST THE LONG ANTIPODEAN SLOTH OF THE SEASON. NOW THE long antipodean hangover. I observe, at last, another year begun. And now try to find the fortnight which has escaped me. The mangroves on the estuary, in this early light, are pale pastures of gold. The house is quiet. It should be some time before anyone wakes. Two women, Irene and sister Beth, currently inhabit the place; I cannot suggest the situation comfortable. But it is a fact. The males in residence, Terror and myself, find refuge here at the desk. The day promises to be another of hard hot brilliance; perhaps we haven't yet exhausted the possibility of picnics on the sand below. Terror has begun to sleep again. I wish I could.

The memory of Beth's arrival is confused by wine and company. She had been uncharacteristically vague about when I should expect her. Tom and Lois were here, making Christmas rounds, and Tony too had dropped in to take a festive glass, and at some time Janet swept in with current amour on her arm, on her way elsewhere. Irene was there, of course, still centre in that haphazard gathering. Then Beth burst in. Glossy, sleek, a shiny suitcase in hand, still an impressive enough figure, indifferent to the desert of the mid-forties; or else in occupation of a well-groomed and amply watered oasis. Her stance never left her status in doubt. Career woman, businesswoman, advertising executive; she made Women's Lib seem a game for giddy girls. She ignored the others, after dismissive glance around, and had words only with me.

'I decided it was time for a family reunion,' she announced. 'Time for the Pikes to foregather. Everyone else is up to that nonsense at this time of year. Why not us too? Anyway I wanted to see how you are. How you really are. For once. It's been years.'

'Yes.' Beth could still overwhelm.

'I expected you to look more romantically wasted. In steady decline. Disappointing. Out here, in the woods, is this the best you can do? And who are all these people?'

'Friends,' I said. 'Plainly.'

'Never mind. At least I've reclaimed my brother. I felt the need. Age, probably. Sentimentality creeping in; first sign of senility. I expected to find you drinking yourself to death, lonely, in a darkened room. What do I find? Lights, music. Hors d'oeuvres on the table. God, I'm starving. Pass me some. Some more of that filthy wine too. Then you can start explaining yourself.'

'It's not the time, Beth. Or the place.'

'It never is. When I think of what I went through, to put you on course, it never ceases to amaze. Why I did it, I mean. Noble self-sacrificing sister; it wasn't me at all. Seeing my raw country brother was comfortable in the city, steering him into the right office, into a safe law degree. Cajoling, consoling. Incredible. And all for what? God knows. What went wrong? You had it made.'

'Possibly,' I allowed.

'It was that singer,' she said. 'That moody bitch. How in hell you muddled into that marriage I'll never know. I can imagine her driving you up the wall.'

'I'm over the wall now. Obviously.'

'Over the wall is out. Don't you remember that game?'

'Indeed.'

'The rule's still good. You're trying to get out of playing. It's not fair on the rest of us.'

'Probably not. You could put in a protest to the umpire.'

'What do you mean? It was just the two of us. We never had an umpire when we played that game.'

'That's what I mean. That's the problem. Nor in this one either.'

'Don't come on large with the metaphysics when I'm around. It won't wash. You always were a lazy little bastard. You'd never have got anywhere, when you came down from the farm, without me pushing. And as soon as you were out of my sight, things started happening. First that marriage. Now this, for God's sake. But it's still laziness, for my money. You're too lazy to cope with yourself or anyone else. The difference now is that you're astute enough to realise it needs some distracting dress. An ideology. But I can see that moony kid on the farm again. No different. Except he now pretends over the wall isn't out.'

'Why do you want me back in the game again?' I asked. 'To make you feel better?'

'There might be something in that,' she allowed honestly. 'I'd feel all my effort wasn't waste.'

'I'm grateful, if that's any help.'

'Not really. I don't need gratitude. I'd be happier to see you doing something profitable with your life.'

'Literally?'

'Literally.'

'In that case it might gratify you to know I've made a couple of thousand dollars in the last month.'

'Then what in hell do you do with it?' She looked around critically. 'Where does it go? You obviously don't spend much doing up this dump. And you don't spend much on this quality booze, surely.' She pulled a face as she swallowed again. 'Sorry to harp; I'll acquire the taste any hour now. Still, you might tell me where the money goes.'

'Into life insurance. Try that for sanity.'

'That's what I mean. You're bloody hopeless.'

'Allow me the benefit of the doubt.'

'I decline to see any benefit. Regretfully. You obviously need someone to keep on your hammer. You married the wrong woman, Paul. She was the snake in the garden. You'd have been better off – well, with someone like me.'

'Very likely,' I tried to agree. 'In one sense. In another, I'm not sorry.'

'You're joking.'

'Just sorry for what went wrong. And not being up to it all. I mean that.'

Perhaps my tone took tougher turn. Anyway she was slow to reply.

'Yes,' she said finally. 'I suppose you do, you poor bastard.'

'So let's call it quits, for tonight anyway. I'm supposed to be host.'

'You'd better steer me around again; I've forgotten their names. Who's that American?'

'Tom Hyde. Pleasant enough. Open.'

'He doesn't look too fascinating. Still, I might chat him up, just to keep my hand in.'

'Well, watch his wife. Lois; on the arm of his chair. She has problems with Tom. I'd sooner, for her sake, you were careful.'

'For your information, Paul, I'm not stupid.'

'That,' I observed, 'wasn't what I was saying.'

'One thing more, as point of interest. I assume that flashy black-haired bird is your woman, if you have one here.'

She meant Janet. 'No. Though Janet and I have been close in spasms.'

'Then who? Not that little hippie creature? She wouldn't say boo to a mouse.'

'She helps me here,' I admitted.

'Helps you?' Beth looked dubious.

'She shows some promise as a potter in her own right. Otherwise she's a good girl Friday.'

'In bed too?'

'In bed too.' It was only hours before that became apparent anyway.

'She looks more like a sad Sunday to me. Is that how it began?'

'I can't remember.'

'Paul, what's happened to you?'

'Strange you should ask.'

'You bastard. Is there any hope of getting through to you?'

I shrugged. 'Probably not,' I answered fairly. 'But you can try.'

She pressed my hand lightly before we moved back across the room. 'Still,' she said, 'we're not too bad, are we? We survive.'

'Yes.'

'More enthusiasm, please.'

'Yes, Beth. We do.'

'Good. You're forgiven.' She seemed to mean it.

Then days of wine, sand, heat and flowering pohutukawa. Too many. Irene wasn't, still isn't, often comfortable. Nor, I suppose, have I been often, with Beth's considerable presence in the place. Irene finds small or no niche in the lengthy dialogues Beth devises to fill her brother's day; Beth mostly insists on overlooking Irene altogether.

There was some relief when Beth began to make evening departures from the house, with no comment or explanation, her tinny mini-rental car stuttering up my difficult drive, leaving a rather satisfying silence in its wake. A fervent house-keeper, enjoying everything in its place, she leaves the house clean and glowing before such departure; Irene and I can be slow moving to establish our own residence here again, guilty lest we leave fleck of food on the stove, spot of wine on the bench, a scrap of tobacco on the floor.

'It isn't the same,' Irene observed unnecessarily.

'No.'

'She thinks you're neglected. She thinks she's looking after you.'

'Very likely. Yes.'

'Perhaps I should go away.'

I thought about that, since I had to. And since I was, no doubt, on test. To reduce complication in my life, and find bare bones again, I had only to say yes. Yes, all right, if you like. And thus make the thing hers. But I couldn't quite. The reason was selfish, it seemed, rather surprisingly. It wasn't just that Irene made buffer against Beth. It wasn't just agitations of flesh and release therefrom. Nothing so functional. Or anything simply. So I made my best, equivocal answer.

'You don't have to,' I said. Then added, 'Beth will be gone soon anyway, if that thought makes you happier.'

'It does,' she said with some force. 'I'm sorry; I know she's your sister; I forget that.'

'I can't,' I said.

'It's just she makes me feel I don't belong. Just when I thought I might after all. People like you and her and your friends, you're all so complicated. It's like watching strange fish in a tank, those tropical ones, all darting and diving, tricky things, with strange colours. And no sound coming through. I really don't know what you're on about, most of the time.'

'About being human, most of the time.'

'But you never say what you mean.'

'Possibly not, if it hurts too much. That's the trick.'

'You were the one who was on about honesty.'

'Metaphorically. I explained that.'

She sighed. 'Well, I expect I'm not a metaphorical kind of person, whatever that is. I'm real. See?' She pinched herself until pain was evident in her trembling eyes. 'I hurt; I can bleed too. No sweat.'

'Agreed.' For some reason I saw Mary Dennis on the roadside again, shiny hair, pale skin, blood everywhere, unwholesomely ambushed.

'Anyway,' she said, reverting to course, 'that sister of yours would be better off with a man. She might leave you alone.'

'She generally is with a man, though I don't think she marries them any longer. She might even be with one now. That doesn't mean she's better off, for the most part. There's need, of course, and reassurance.'

'There you are. You're going back into that tank again, all tricky. Why don't you just come right out and say she needs a fuck now and then?'

This upset me slightly; I wasn't sure why. 'Because I don't think it's always that simple.'

'Or because you don't want it to be that simple?'

'I don't think this gets us anywhere,' I announced.

'Because it's about your sister?'

'No. Because I think it's time we fetched up a couple of spears, and a lamp, and tried the estuary for flounder at night. We haven't this summer, not yet.'

'You make it sound as if we've had other summers.'

'Do I?' Possibly I sounded surprised.

'I expect there'll only be the one,' she said. 'So I'd better make the best of it.'

I saw no point in contradicting her, if she so virginally wished to wed the likely truth; it might make things lighter later, the bleeding less. Not that I cared to think. I fetched spears and lamp from the junk cupboard in the kitchen, and we went together to the outside door. Terror jerked awake and followed.

'Do we take him?' she asked.

'No. Shut him in the house.'

'Why? He'll be lonely.' She knelt to pat his head.

'He'll get frisky and scare the flounder off. Spoil things. It's pure peace down there at night. You see.'

It was. The dark tide under the stars; the shiny threads of light across the water spun by waterside homes; overhanging branches bulking suddenly out of the night. Most sensation was tactile. Sand, then mud and shells underfoot; and the warm sea as we began to wade. The lamp hissed in my hand. Its yellow glow conjured strange magnified shapes, wavering things of dream, from the lucid water: weeds, twigs, rocks, crabs, tiny fish, a dazzled eel; all manner of intricate and honest substance. And then a rippling trail of mud rose as our first flounder swerved away.

'Goodbye breakfast,' I observed. 'They're what we watch for now.' I tried to concentrate on sight of their furtive shape; Irene kept abreast of the light as I stalked. The night was soundless, aside from the light splash of sea on our limbs.

'I love you,' she said.

'What's that?' I offered not to hear.

She tried again. 'I just said I love you.'

'Don't,' I said quick.

'Why not?'

'Because you're here on a promise of peace.'

'And that kills it?'

'Something like that.'

'Next time perhaps you'd better shut me inside with Terror. So you can get on with the peace bit. Sorry if it's not your bag. Not fair, am I?'

'I'm no judge.'

'Your sister is. At least she thinks so. She told me yesterday that if I thought I meant anything to you, then I better grow up fast. So it looks like I should do that. And take my place in the tank.'

'Let's have some quiet,' I protested. 'We'll never find flounder this way.'

She sniffed, and sidled away towards the shore. But after a time she returned. I skewered three flounder, one after another, in sudden succession, and flipped them from the water to flap in the bucket she held.

'There,' I said. 'One each. Enough.'

'You make it easy.'

'Given reasonable peace. Yes.'

'Sorry then. I'll try harder to fit.'

She moved against me in the dark as we reached the dry shore. Lamp, spears and other appurtenances of our expedition were set on the sand. She became again a shy and shaky thing in my arms; her legs soon gave way, and I went down with her. At the edge of the lamplight, then, I unpeeled her light clothing with method, while she gasped and grappled with the firm flesh I offered, and finally found herself fitting with some satisfaction. No real effort at all. She could always offer surprising shapes; it was never less than sustaining. When her urgencies were diminished, I concentrated on the climax of my own need, and that was as swift and restorative as ever. Technically, at least, the triumph was pure; nothing left undone, our senses sated. We heard the light slap of sea on rock again, saw stars in the sky beyond elaborately overprinted foliage; the beach had fine trembling yellow glaze of light from our lamp, the sand richly corrugated with shadows.

'Yes,' she said suddenly. 'Yes.'

I didn't ask her to explain that affirmation. A slow-dying flounder flapped in the bucket.

Beth arrived back this morning at first light, an hour or two ago. She woke me, in fact, when her car had an argument with some foliage and fern while she backed it awkwardly, perhaps drunkenly, down the drive. Then she went heavily through the house to her single bed. Perhaps she has found some old suitor in the city to give her satisfaction; Beth has old suitors everywhere, never further than the nearest telephone. Since I don't have one, she makes use of the call-box at the corner.

I waited until reasonably sure she was sleeping. Then I rose, went quiet and barefoot through the house, and recovered these journals for the first time this year. And perhaps not before time.

I feel the need of clay again. I think I shall find my feet in the pit this morning. And later, beside the wheel. There is no consolation elsewhere.

January 5, 1892: Thirty years now since I became Castaway in this Country, in search of New Life, & more than ten I see since I made more than scant entry here. The anniversary of the first occasion – New Year's Day in truth – has near enough escaped me, though I try late to rectify the omission now. Thirty years in all. The thought is Terrifying & enough to wither me, as age is trying to do, & I feel this pen tremble in my grip as I write it down. Three decades unravel & each strand leads only to another & convinces me that it does not do to pick at One's life too much or often lest all things fall apart & tumble down, leaving only a hole where a man has been under God's sky, an empty space once full of fancies. I do not have many wild Fancies now. Why should I, in truth? My acres are green & solid enough. My fat animals graze. My homestead, final fruit of my endeavours here, testimony to Life anew, is long finished & undeniably a place of substance among these huge trees now green with summer leaf & will long outlive me & perhaps my Children. Also I have not been Alone in the end. My wife Florence may have her Bitter Moments, for she is always aware of my Inadequacies as Husband & perhaps as man, but still she has always had Wifely virtue in plenty & I have never lacked for her attentions. Our daughter Mary, the name I chose above others of Florence's suggestion, thus obstinately prevailing for once in our discussions, is now a most sturdy seven years old & though not yet beyond childish tantrum is generally a pleasant good girl not unlike Florence in appearance & also not in the sharp way of her tongue when she sometimes speaks to me in anger, as Children will. But still I would not wish that precious little creature to be other, for she is all I have. Also it is still not impossible that I shall have a Son, to preserve the name Pike in this place, for Florence has begun to flourish again with late pregnancy & in three months or four I shall know what Fate gives me in last throw. I might be less lonely with a Son & less inclined to walk aimlessly outdoors when seasonal tasks are slack, though at the age of fifty-five Years now I must confess myself ill situated to enjoy his maturity as man & see what becomes of him here. All I may do, before drawing Last Breath, is wish him well on his way & hope his Journey will take strength from mine & make more sense in the end. I should tell him perhaps that a man best puts Dreams away, possibly wrapped in tough canvas beneath a Floorboard, along with other childish & youthful Fevers. And treats Life, as Florence would have it, as Business Proposition, with Gospel backing or no, if not quite at such extreme. That way might bring a contented Pike, with all things making sense in the End.

Did it? I consider that unborn child and then contemplate the corpse of my father again as it rests in memory beside his unfinished fence. My widowed mother and freshly fatherless sister weep beside me. Neighbours are gathering him up and placing him on a sledge, to be towed away. Memory still allows me sight of his face, however, with all the distractions. I find a scar on his forehead, a bullet graze from Gallipoli; and a congealed cut on his jaw from shaving that morning. There is also a mud-stain from falling face down on the wintry earth he had trodden to mush while fixing the fence, framing the Pike acres. What I fail to find in that face, though, is content; and sense in his End. I looked away then. I look away now.

I think it time, surely, to proceed with frying the flounder for breakfast. They may serve to sustain the Business Proposition. And later the clay.

11

January 17:

THE SHELVES FILL SLOWLY. BUT I AM AFTER ALL WORKING for myself again; Tom Hyde should now have sufficient cheques to see him through. I don't ask for account of how the money is spent, so long as it lubricates his enthusiasm to save the estuary from hurt. Insofar as we have conversed lately, he tells me all is quiet on the battle front at the moment; the ecology is safe in the customary rigor mortis of January's heat. To which I offer only a compulsive twitch or two, in the shade of the lean-to, while I can. Irene finds shelter there too. This slack season hasn't stolen the lessons she learned. I like her confidence at the wheel. She even seems an inch or two taller, at times. Imagination, of course; perhaps the confidence too. But I could imagine worse.

The earth smells dry; breezes make arid rattles in the bush; the garden grabs water by the gallon. But the tomatoes are huge, the capsicums burgeoning, and the cucumber makes cool salads for our table. The red festive flush of flower along the estuary has faded; the greens grow lacklustre.

While I work on the wheel, Irene now often fidgets with clay on her own account. She produces flat shapes, hearts, diamonds, with tiny twined figures in relief; they are not without interest. What, I asked, were they?

Dreams, she said. Hopes.

I made no comment. I just offer to put them through the fire.

Beth has some time departed. In the end her visit wasn't without incidental drama. There was, for example, battering on my door in the middle of the night, long after Irene and I had gone to bed. And Terror barking in berserk fashion. My first thought, oddly, was that the tribe of Daniels might have descended to claim back their own; and Irene's reaction might not have been dissimilar, for she grew quite stiff with panic. And said, 'Don't answer.'

The battering began again. The barking didn't diminish.

'It could be anyone,' I insisted, wholly woken. 'We can't leave it.'

I pulled a lavalava respectably about my trunk, and travelled through the darkness to the door. Before I opened it, though, I switched on a light as precaution. And held Terror back, like a catapult ready to fire.

It was, after all, Lois Hyde. Wild-eyed and dripping from nocturnal summer shower. I called Terror to heel. Otherwise she didn't allow me time to speak.

'Where are they?' she shouted. 'Where the hell are they?'

'Who? What's wrong, Lois? Come in. Who do you want?'

'Tom,' she announced. 'And that crafty bitch of a sister of yours.'

She tumbled past me, into the house, perhaps in imaginary pursuit. But Beth was out, and I hadn't seen Tom in a week.

'What's the trouble?' I asked, though it was already clear.

'They're on together. Don't you know?'

'No, Lois. I didn't. I'm sorry.'

'They're not here?'

'No.'

She began to deflate. 'Then where the hell are they?'

'I've no idea. You sure about it all, though?'

'I'm no fool. I usually know what Tom's up to. And who with.'

With this pronouncement, however, she began weeping loudly. I pulled off her coat, and guided her to a chair. Irene didn't stir from our bedroom, but I could imagine her listening.

'It's been one damn thing after another,' Lois sobbed. 'One sexy bitch after another. You must know what Tom's like lately. Is this what men are when they hit forty? No one warned me. I can't go on like this. I swear it, I can't.'

'Look, Lois –' I began. And then felt at perplexing loss about where to guide her gaze in consolation.

'You're not like that. You're not carrying on all the time. Why should Tom?'

Tom, perhaps, was married. But that might not be tactfully said. 'We're different, possibly,' I suggested. 'I'm free and not inclined to do much about it. Whereas Tom may be chafing. Patience, Lois. He'll come down to earth again. You see. A matter of time.'

A string of perfect platitudes unwinding. I had to stop before I choked.

At least the sobs subsided. She grew serenely bitter. 'In that case I begin to think I won't be around when he floats down to earth from cloud nine or wherever. Nor his kids. The hell with waiting. I'll pack up and go home and leave him to his brave new life.'

I considered a coffee interval reasonably relevant. First, though, I gave Lois a large whisky. She gulped it thirstily, like weak beer. While coffee warmed, I argued, 'Tom loves his kids; you too. That's why he brought you all out here in the first instance, as I recall. So you'd all have a better chance in

148

some green uncluttered place. It would kill him if you did that.'

'So it would kill him,' she said flatly. 'And who cares?'

'I do. I care for you both.'

But I also, I began to discern, cared for Tom's campaign to save the estuary; and I didn't care to imagine that collapsing obscurely among matrimonial ruin. This thought, plus my investment, lent certain urgency to the scene.

'Then talk to him,' she said. 'Tell him to pull himself together. And tell your sister to lay off too.'

'I'm not my sister's keeper. But I'll try to do what I can. And I'll talk to Tom.' The least I could promise. 'That's if you agree to do nothing rash in the meantime.'

'I keep my options open,' Lois insisted.

'Just in the meantime,' I repeated.

'All right, I won't rush off. Not yet.'

'Give things a month or two to settle. Then see how you feel.'

'All right,' she sighed.

'Good,' I said with relief. 'Now how about coffee?'

'I shouldn't unload all this on to you,' she said judiciously. 'After all, it's not your doing. And if it wasn't your sister, it would be someone else. At least she's transient.'

'It's all a phase.' I shuffled through platitudes again and dealt the first likely.

'So I tell myself. Not that it helps much, most of the time. It's just hell, Paul. Hell.'

'Yes,' I said shakily. 'I expect it is.'

'Because I still care for him. Terribly. That's the hell, you see. And the kids adore him, perhaps because he's such a big overgrown kid himself. He can't even tell me a good lie, when he has to. The worst thing is, I know he'd go to pieces without me; he'd be no use to anyone.'

He might, of course, also grow up; and Lois, if she reasonably called quits, might have less hell. But I quickly checked that thought. 'All the more reason, then,' I said mildly, 'to hang on to what you feel for him, in the meantime. Go on. Try to go on. See if things settle.' At this point, however, I seemed to have confused saving the Hyde marriage and life as they lived it with saving the estuary and life as I lived it; God knew. I hoped the coffee, which I was now spiking liberally with whisky, might take the slightly sour taste in my mouth away. Lois was grateful for it anyway. She smiled bravely, still moist eyed, as she sipped. She might have made more of her attractions as a woman, if lumbered with a husband less a liability. She might also have been more of a person, without his solicitous siring of so many children; she wasn't unintelligent either. If she called quits now, she might be more; but who was I to play God and say? At least the hazard in the status quo was known and not beyond taming; elsewhere dwelled dragons. Onward the status quo then. A pleasing piece of rationalisation? I might never know. I surrendered, like Lois, to the heady coffee.

Afterwards, and after less taxing talk, I walked her up the leafy road home. Beth's car, thank God, didn't pass us on the way. At her gate she crushed against me and kissed my cheek. 'You won't come in?' she asked.

'No. Perhaps not.'

'That girl's still with you? That quiet one?'

'Yes. She was there tonight.' Since that was an excuse Lois could understand, with no pride lost.

'Pity. So all I can do is say thanks.'

'Something like that. But you don't have to.'

'But I do, you see. Thank you, Paul. For being patient. For everything.' She kissed my cheek again, and drifted away into the dark.

Another shower caught me on the way home, distinctly cooling. Irene, as I feared, was awoken still. The bedside lamp was on; the cigarette smoke thick.

'That,' she announced, 'was like a horror story.'

150

'It wasn't pleasant,' I agreed.

'That poor woman. Do you have to carry on that way, all of you? There's no honesty at all.'

'Well –' I felt tired.

'It made me sick,' she declared. 'Just listening, it made me sick.'

'I wasn't a picture of health either.'

'No wonder. You were no help to her. Just go on, you told her. Just go on. What for?'

'Indeed,' I said. 'But people do.' I was more interested in sleep than argument, but she persisted.

'You were telling her, really, to be dishonest about her real feelings. And it just made me sick.'

'We've had that line,' I said, weary.

'The whole scene was sad and sick.'

'I've become familiar with other sad sick scenes lately.'

'You're talking about mine.'

'If you like.' I didn't mean to press it.

'At least there was some honesty. Even in the things that shocked you.'

'Oh?'

'That time I told you about, for example, the time I was in bed with four men. I know that upset you; I could see. But at least it was honest. They were honest about what they wanted. And so was I. So we weren't hurting anyone, were we?'

'It's a viewpoint,' I conceded.

'No one freaked out. No one wept and yelled and banged on doors in the middle of the night. No one felt life wasn't worth it. Not because of that; never.'

'All right, so Lois was unhappy. I think we've established that. Now, can we let it rest?'

'No,' she said. 'I can't.'

'Hell's teeth.' I slumped heavily on the edge of the bed. 'What more do you want?'

'Something better than what I've seen. Is that too much to ask?'

'Yes,' I said. 'Probably.'

'Are you really past caring?'

'At the moment, yes. It's going on for four in the morning. Try me in daylight.'

'I have. It's really no better.'

'God help us.' It was a genuine plea.

'Truth should be more than talk.'

'Agreed. And it is. Wherever it is.'

'I mean truth between people.'

'That's out of the question. We all speak different languages. That's our original curse. Individual consciousness. But for the sake of simple convenience we spend most of our lives pretending that it isn't so. That we can understand each other.'

'So what's the answer?'

'If it's out of the question, then there is no answer.'

'You're right about one thing. You certainly don't understand me.'

'No. Probably not.' I was wrestling with the request of sleep now.

'Or her. That woman; Lois.'

'No.' I was ready to submit all along the line.

'She came to you for more than the consolation you gave.'

'Possibly,' I agreed. Anything to get it over.

'But you couldn't face that, could you? Not really. You just talked about helping her. But in the crunch you chickened out.'

'It wasn't an easy situation.'

'If you mean you're fussy about my feelings, forget it. I'd have understood. I could have just moved over in bed, or even lent a hand. Or you could have taken her to your sister's; that would have been interesting. Or to hers. I wouldn't have minded. I'd have understood.'

'No doubt.'

'Don't make fun of me. Whatever you do, don't do that.'

'You were asking for honesty.'

'Making fun of people is running away from it.'

'All right then. Under the old rules of the game, going to bed with someone generally meant something. So some of us still feel the need of guidelines, even indifferently and erratically painted ones. And if they're no longer there, we pretend they are. Take Lois now, since you insist. All those lives at issue.'

'But you were thinking of yours.'

'Not unreasonably. I can do without Lois frantic at my door in the middle of the night. Is that enough honesty for this hour? Can I go to sleep now?' I climbed into bed beside her and switched off the light.

There was silence for a time.

Then, beginning to drown in sleep, I heard her say, 'If going to bed with someone means something, like you said, what does this mean to you? Going to bed with me?'

'I can do without questions like that in the middle of the night too.'

'When else are you going to get them?'

'All right. The answer is, I don't know.'

'Or you don't want to know.'

'I don't know.' That was honesty, if she liked; and without ferocious flaw. I slept. Perhaps she did too. I didn't even hear Beth get in.

The bed, when I woke, was empty of Irene; the house too. I felt sudden and unmistakable tremor until I found my way to a window, looked out, and then with relief saw her at a distance, engaged with clay under the lean-to. She had Terror tied there too, for company. Pleasant to know someone found purpose in the morning. It also left me free for a clear run at Beth when she stirred. And this she did, eventually, while I was breakfasting. In shimmery blue gown she went through

153

to the kitchen, poured coffee into a large mug, managed to salvage some unburned bread from my tired toaster, and then came to sit at the table beside me.

'So I imagine you had a more satisfying night than I did,' I observed. Quite coolly, considering.

'It had its moments,' she agreed. 'One or two.'

'I had Tom's wife here, you see. Lois.'

'Conventionally distraught?'

'Yes. Unsurprisingly.'

'I'm sorry for you.'

'I'm sorry for Lois. I wish you wouldn't.'

'Oh dear.' She sighed.

'Just a holiday fling, is it?'

'Of course. Even down to the obscure beach hideaway. Of his arranging, not mine.'

'That's something, I expect. Not much, but something.'

'That's about what it boils down to. Not much, but something. I wouldn't call it an elegant encounter. Not with Tom and that decrepit sin bin by the beach. All sex for beginners, really. An amiable bull at a gate. A certain amount of enviable gusto, I admit. But needing more oblique direction to be useful.'

'I don't think I want to know, thanks all the same.'

'Still as fastidious as ever.'

'Always, over breakfast.'

'I've become an embarrassment to you. Is that it? You'd like me to leave.'

'Not necessarily,' I said. 'It depends on you.'

'I'm leaving in a day or two anyway. I've done my bit. The Pikes have once again foregathered to their mutual dismay. Perhaps for the last time. Think on it, brother.'

'No problem.'

'I'm sorry my sex life should have become intrusive to the point of earning your explicit disapproval. But still, I don't

154

see yours as spectacularly healthy either, if you don't mind me saying so.'

'I do mind you saying. It's beside the point.'

'Possibly. But I can't help noticing, can I? It's just one extreme to the other. First of all you're on with a somebody; at least I can say that of Anna. Now you're on with an absolute nobody. What is it then? Do you feel obliged to make some retrospective apology for celebrity-seeking? Tell me; all most intriguing.'

'I'm not on with anyone, as it happens. Otherwise I reserve defence.'

'She shares your bed, I note. Is it a penance then? Or is it just that she offers no large affront to your ego?'

'For God's sake, Beth, give it a bone.' An expression I hadn't used in years; a good farm phrase.

'Which offers one clue,' she veered on with aplomb. 'You wanted someone to toss a bone of wisdom to now and then. To keep that smelly dog company, in this mildewed place. At one with Paul Pike's new life style – down in the mouth, down at heel, down in the world; down, down, down. How's that for starters? You couldn't have gone down any deeper for her.'

'Beth, I think I'm about to lose my temper.'

'So we'll do the full family reunion bit. Why not?'

'Because it's not my inclination.'

'You think it's a farce, this talk of family.'

'In a way,' I agreed.

'Tragedy always repeats itself as farce, I read somewhere.'

'The Pikes aren't tragic enough.'

'Then perhaps it's the other way round. Farce repeats itself as tragedy. Now tell me we aren't farcical enough. The last of us. Me childless, waiting on the menopause to ride high-hatted on the horizon. And you – ' She paused and took a look at my face, which seemed to prove enough. 'Well, never mind. It doesn't matter. Sorry. While I think to say it, though, don't go getting the silly little bitch pregnant. The Pikes don't need propagation that badly. It would be both tragedy and farce, so far as you're concerned. Look up a bit, Paul. Take pride in yourself.'

'You're an old fashioned snob, Beth.'

'And why not? What did holy squalor ever make? Just more of the same.'

'I've no pretence to holiness. And the squalor's a matter of opinion.'

'But the way you live – ' she began.

'Is just the way I live. An experiment in sanity. It doesn't suit you. But it demonstrably suits me. Now, can we leave it?'

Beth left anyway, next day, slightly sooner than promised. We'd used up our ammunition; the end was amiable after all, and the Pike reunion at rest. Tragedy, farce? The Pikes could never aspire to either; and nor perhaps their country. I took a large breath of it, anyway, when she'd gone. First literally, out on my porch, with a great mug of beer: a day of green and blue, the bulky hills sea-invaded under the sun. Then more metaphorically at my desk. 'Keeping accounts again?' said Irene, passing through the room.

March 31, 1892: Early this a.m. a male child born to Florence & self. A difficult birth & much sweat & pain & fear, but he survives & shall. I cannot doubt this for an instant. I walked restless through the house almost until dawn after this Miracle was announced. Then as the Dark lightened I climbed a hill towards Sunrise & as those first gleams of Gold garnished the grey shapes of morning all around I fell fervently on my knees & gave thanks to God & much praise to His fairness & promised myself & Him always to be worthy of His wisdom. I had not thought myself such a religious fellow before. Nor when I rose from that situation with ache in my knees had the world shown itself to me so purely before. All creation was a resplendent thing. The sky & the ferns & the spiky palms & the tiniest things around me & the separate blades of grass. I felt at One with my own domain & thankful to God for the things I have wrought here. The slender view of the sea which the furthest horizon allowed me, where the edge of this untidy country disperses into bays & islands, beckoned my Thought to higher things, no small mercy. For I confess now to having recently grubbed too long among petty grievances about this country my son will doubtless call his own but which I still cannot unless with effort. Of late I have not thought it worthy of my efforts after all as if it & not myself were to blame for what I am or have been & as if it had in some measure cheated me of youth & manhood in return for nothing much. But the harvest of the seed I have sown so long in Florence's unwilling womb has transformed all & shown exile & patience may have reward. For I could rejoice in my Life not just as thing in itself but also for where I have planted it among these stubborn hills & in these lonely islands at the World's edge & think with Vision regained of what shall be & what roads here the Pikes shall travel & what pleasures they after all shall take from Life in so quiet a place at vast remove from the large sounds & commotions & miseries of the outer world. I could see, as though some veil had fallen, that what I & others have been about here & trust not all will have been in vain. I set this down in haste lest Life envelop me too soon in coarse textures, the drab dull garment of the daily round again. Yet I know all the same that only Death, when he chooses to take me, will really rob me of the wonder of this dawn I have known & he shall in consequence have to fight for my last heartbeat & find nothing easy. I may have regrets about Life & my lost love & failures but they shall be as nothing now & he shall not use despair as lever to free my soul of Flesh. I would only that I had someone to share all this with, in truth, but perhaps this wish is of no great moment, so long as I can set it down for myself & for someone who may one day share. Who am I now to complain or grieve. Mary my daughter has this moment looked over my shoulder & asked what I am doing & with the glow of the day I took her upon my knee. She is a bony cold thing & would not have much business with the affection I offered & soon wriggled free running upstairs to where her mother is abed & thus leaving me to reflect for a time on why I had named her so. Perhaps a thing of no real Import & not to be puzzled over since I am only a man. Florence well.

Keeping accounts? Of course. Double entry book-keeping, no less.

More fish are running. Irene and I manoeuvre the mullet net into place, awash to our waists, and sometimes drag it up the estuary when the tide is clearing fast.

Possibly I shall have sufficient pots for a firing in another week or two. Also some dreams, hopes. Beth's visit has left certain silences in its wake; and at least one unanswered question. Perhaps a thing of no real Import & not to be puzzled over since I am only a man.

Otherwise Irene well. Perhaps Tom and Lois again too; at least no further consequences batter upon my door.

I look back through pages, with faint and fading hope that an answer will take me unawares, but the accounts appear too accurately kept. Better to walk outside perhaps, down the track, where fantails flirt among the foliage and the season, like all seasons, seems answerable only to itself.

Irene told me I used Anna's name while talking, mostly incoherently, in my sleep last night.

'And who is Charlie?' she asked.

12

February 17:

A FULL MONTH GONE, IT SEEMS. WE STILL INHABIT THE STICKY climax of summer. The year still runs in low gear, often drifting in no more than neutral. Perhaps only Irene gives it erratic impetus. The garden is dense with vegetables, aubergines, capsicums, cucumbers, beans; time to bottle and pickle. And I have, on the whole, more fish than I can give away.

In this heat I crave the cool of autumn. Even the fresh and frosty winds of winter. Grey sky and rain bring no relief; the moisture rises humidly from the growth around.

Account for the month? Too painless, perhaps: there is no temptation. I could, this easily, let a year slip past. Or years altogether. No sweat. Even in this heat.

Beth has written a belated bread and butter note. Saying thanks, brother, and little more. The jam, if any, was in her last sentence 'We are what we are, I suppose, never much more; I'm sorry.'

Out of sight, sister. Right out of sight. For I think she shall be. I have made no reply.

I begin to gather the first harvest of the year for Janet's disposal; and include a handful of Irene's intricacies. She refuses to serve the functional; she is off on her own. And entirely absorbed within what she does. Dreams, hopes? She is not inclined to be specific. I simply see all her conceits are fired safely.

Otherwise I do not search the season for flaw.

Even Tom Hyde is, for once, optimistic. He thinks Rangiwai will live; at least that the estuary will survive. The uproar is growing, he insists, however little I hear of it here. The planners and bureaucrats are running scared. Not least, he explains, because the legal representations have been so impressive, purchased by Pike's pots; an immaculate bargain.

'I've a confession to make, though,' he added.

'Oh?'

'There's all kinds of money flowing in now. All kinds of influence.'

'I see.'

'I hate to admit it, but a fight's a fight. One can't always pick and choose allies.'

'What are you getting at?'

'If you must know, we've got all kinds of developers and speculators behind us suddenly. They see a threat to their investments on the peninsula if the estuary's fouled. They've been buying up steadily and quietly around here for the last year. Riding the ecology kick, you see. They see the peninsula as an elegant back-to-nature suburb for executives. It's all on the drawing board already. Logical, if you think about it, a forgotten corner like this. Once despised. Now desirable. Not difficult to understand.'

'No.'

160

'Their money's welcome. And their pressure. Once we've fought the bureaucrats, we'll have to turn around and fight them. To keep them from wrecking the place too. But it's tactics right now. First things first. You see what I mean?'

'I'm trying.'

Daniels still keeps his distance. Most things do.

Once a week, roughly, I take a drink with Tony and Rose. We look down on the sea; they recall their past; we joke. I see Rose as fast growing feebler. She seldom enters her garden now; weeds flourish among the flowers. Does Tony notice? Possibly. But we don't talk of it. So long as Rose remains in the flesh, he won't complain. I give him no cause for complaint. I make no observation about Rose. And the weeds grow.

Irene, on the beach today, after a long swim: 'I should be happy, I expect.'

I advanced no opinion.

'It bugs me when I'm not. Everything's good, really, when I think about it. I'm safe, aren't I?'

'Of course.'

'Don't say of course. Tell me I am.'

'You're safe. How's that?'

'So it's silly to wish for more, isn't it?'

'People do.'

'I mean,' she went on, 'there's only one thing wrong here. But it's silly to wish you loved me.'

A small blight, things considered. But possibly sufficient to drive me to this desk again.

Perhaps Irene has found the flaw.

'I need to be loved, I think,' she added. 'I wish I didn't. It's just it might make me more safe. But I wish I didn't.'

Back up at the house, afterwards, I opened a fresh flagon.

No need to pretend it an answer. There isn't one. Or in bed. Neither here nor elsewhere.

August 5, 1897: I encounter my sixty-first Year with some surprise today & no little vexation. I should from the vantage point my sixty years offer now be able to take stock of my life & see it true but the Shop seems empty. So much then for Business Propositions. I may it seems live out this Century after all but as an old tired man with a son too young & tender to be true Companion of that twilight. This day was one of bitter Weather & though long sheltered inside & dry by the evening fire I can still feel the chill rain in my bones & a cough shakes my thin ribs so that I cannot even take comfort in tobacco as I sit here with the house quiet around me. I cannot even find the customary things to say about my Life & my visions are bleak. I live with a woman who is but a stranger & a daughter not much more & a Son I may never know. Perhaps the evil trick Life plays upon us is the whisper in our ear that things could have been different than they are. That whisper in my ear & that dream might have had the name of Mary but I shall never know & shall soon doubtless be too old & cold to care for more than the Comfort a warm fire may offer. Perhaps I shall soon enter with relief upon that senile bliss, the Demons dead who long nagged me & all restless things gone. I feel large need emptying from my Flesh already & Florence alas in the way of women has preceded me in that Regard. I had best consign this feeble Chronicle to its grave beneath the floorboards before I say anything further I may regret. Would that it were never found again & would that I had the Courage of my Convictions to toss it into the fire rather than let rats & damp & time do the work I cannot bring myself to do.

Alas, his canvas shroud proved too durable for any posthumous consolation; it remained intact, the pages showing only faint yellow patina of age, until the floorboards were levered up, in the course of renovation, long after the Pikes were parted from their Eden. It found its way to me late, perhaps, but not too late. I can at least be seen as one who is not too young & tender to be true Companion of that twilight. With peace as my plea.

I think it time to try the sea again. Irene, behind me, has just attempted to replace a record on the player.

'No,' I said, when it began. 'Not that one.'

'Why?' she asked. Dismayed. 'I was looking for something you liked. And you often played this one when I first came.'

'Not today,' I said. 'Not now.'

'Why get upset? It's only music.'

True. A mere whisper in the ear.

13

March 14:

I THOUGHT I FELT COOLING IN THE AIR WHEN I BEGAN THE DAY.
An illusion, doubtless; a trick of hope; the sweat was still thick
on my face when I worked on the wheel up to noon. Then I
went out into the garden, for a time, to battle bugs and blight.
The tomatoes are blotched already, and the cucumbers in
considerable disrepair. The tideless estuary offered no relief
from the heat. When I returned to the house I found Irene indifferent and listless again; she had preferred not to join me
under the lean-to. I have not questioned this recent mood; I
prefer not to observe it. Possibly she suspects Janet's reaction
to her work.

'Sentimental crap,' Janet said. 'What do you think you're up
to? Don't tell me you're going this way on me. You don't
expect me to take this junk seriously.'

'Look again,' I suggested.

'I just have,' she said. 'Kid stuff. No thanks.'

Irene, fortunately, was out of earshot, as she usually is
when Janet is about.

'I begin to see,' Janet said suddenly. 'It's not yours at all.'

I acknowledged this.

'Well.' She paused. 'Tell the kid I'm sorry. I can see she's tried hard. But I have to set some standard in the shop. You can see that, can't you?'

'Of course,' I agreed.

'It's too bad, really. I wish I could offer some hope. Why don't you try her on the wheel?'

'I have.'

'And?'

'She was coming on. But she preferred to find her own thing. Decorative.'

'Fine if it keeps her happy.'

'Indeed. I hoped it would.'

'So what about you? I'm trying hard to see you as happier. I'm still not sure.'

'Irrelevant.'

'I wish it were. Most quixotic, taking her in. No doubt it's done her good. But what's it doing for you? Or to you?'

'Another interest in life. Often said necessary past forty.'

'Come on, now.'

'She's all right here. No great hazard.'

'So you'd like to think.'

'Naturally.'

'You are a stubborn bastard.'

'Up to a point. I know which point.'

'You simply don't want to know how people tick.'

'Not much, no. It only leads to wondering why they do at all. The fact is that they do, despite most things. I can accept that now without great effort; it took me some time. Don't ask too much more.'

'Sorry. So I won't ask. How did we get on this tack anyway? I only meant to mention Anna.'

'Do you have to?'

'I think so. For someone's sake. Hers; yours. Or my own. God knows. I can't just say nothing, can I?'

'Go on, then.' I looked up, briefly, to see if some cloud had crossed the sun. None had; the day was obstinately bright. And hot. I was sweating again.

'It isn't much really. Just that I've seen her fairly frequently of late. She's been rehearsing, you see, in a hall near the shop. And she tends to pass by, or through, afterwards. Just browsing, mostly. Not buying. No guess where she gives her attention. Anyway I sometimes make her coffee, and she seems grateful enough for that. And a chance to talk.'

'I see. Well, thanks for telling me.'

'You're hardly mentioned, if that's what's bugging you. She still never does more than ask quietly if you're all right. To which I say yes. That's all.'

'And she's all right?' I tried not to ask.

'Calm. Calmer than I've seen her before. The work, no doubt; the challenge. Though she's some reason to be nervous now, with opening night only a couple of weeks away. She's been unsure whether she's up to it. That's what she talks about, mostly. How things are going. Not about you at all. In any case – ' She hesitated.

'Yes? In any case?'

'I'm not sure how I should phrase this, or if I should.'

'Try.'

'Well, in any case I have a feeling there may be someone else.'

'Not before time, then.' There was relief, clearly; but also a deeper reverberation. I hoped Janet saw only the first.

'She mentions this tenor. The one she's working with. Not with great emphasis; he just crops up now and then as she talks. But I notice. I don't know whether I'm meant to. Knowing Anna, even if meagrely, I doubt it. I just do, that's all. Perhaps I'm jumping to conclusions and shouldn't have mentioned him. Sorry, if so.'

166

'Well,' I said, 'is it all over now? Or is there more to come?'

'No,' she answered. 'It's all over. Relax, Paul. I just thought it might be consolation; I can see I'm a fool.' She put out a hand; it fell light on my arm. Her gaze was frank and perhaps fond. Eventually I avoided it. But the hand remained. 'All right?' she asked presently.

'All right.' I was tempted to be brusque; I wasn't.

'Anyway your work's going well; those new glazes are extraordinary. As for sales, if that matters, there's been no slackening off this year. You're riding a boom. I'm just sorry about these.' She indicated Irene's pieces again.

So I purchased them from my own pocket in the end, paid Irene, and hid them in the house. Dreams, hopes. Perhaps she found them hidden. They should properly have gone under a floorboard. I find myself reluctant, otherwise, to explain her mood.

Silly to wish for more? But people do. They do. Even when safe; even when surviving. However sweet the flesh of the apple, they still insist on finding the worm within. We still make love often, if that is the word; at least we manage to manufacture something satisfying, for a time, upon bed or beach or couch. If not love, then the next best thing; why wish more? But we do. The whisper; the worm. God help us all.

Anyway I was still helpless. After lunch I took retreat in the garden again. Irene silently walked Terror away through the trees; she was gone some time. Perhaps just finding tracks and following them.

It seemed better that night; better in bed. Until the knocking again, the barking. What now? I could only think a repeat performance from Lois; Tom Hyde on some randy rampage again. And me to explain and console. My imagination went no further as I tugged on gown rather than lavalava, since the night now had decided coolness. I went to the door, held Terror back, opened it, and then confronted demand of a different kind. For Tony stood there, in clear distress, with grey hair awry, and frightened eyes. Terror quit barking and licked his legs.

'It's Rose,' he said. As if I needed to be told.

'Yes.'

'There's a doctor coming, an ambulance. But I think she's going. Can you be with me? I don't think I can take it alone.' He was almost apologetic.

'Of course, Tony. Of course I can come.'

He hurried back to his house. I returned to the bedroom and began dressing swiftly.

'Who knocked?' asked Irene from the bed.

'Death, most likely. With a gentle face.'

'What are you talking about? Who?' Wrong to unnerve her; too late.

'My neighbour. Tony. His wife's in trouble.'

'Not another one.' She seemed confused. Not unreasonably.

'It's not a question of infidelity, not this time. Or perhaps it is.' I pulled a sweater over my head. 'It seems she's dying, you see.'

'And you have to go?'

'Yes.' I laced boots.

'How long will I be alone?' She never liked that.

'God knows. It's not at my disposal. Anyway you've got Terror here. His entire devotion.'

'Yes. That's about all. I can see that now.'

'Don't make things difficult.'

'I don't have to,' she answered.

'At least,' I observed, 'I don't keep you prisoner. Or is that what you want?'

Her voice cracked. 'I don't know what I want.'

'Too bloody true.' I was impatient now.

'I think I just want to be loved. And safer.'

'For God's sake. Not now.'

'I'm afraid. I'm dying too. Think of that.'

'Who isn't?' It had to end.

'You can't save her. You can save me.'

'Not now.'

'You could pretend to love me. Would that hurt?'

'Yes. Because then I might.'

'You mean you could?' There was a tremor of hope.

'No,' I shouted, angry now. 'No, for God's sake.'

She was about to weep. 'Do you have to go?'

'Yes. Because there's something I understand out there. The rest, never.'

She did weep then.

'I'm sorry.' The least I could say.

'Go on,' she said. 'Go.'

I managed that without hesitation. I left her for the dark outside, and followed Tony up through the ferns to Rose's bedside, cruelly lit. Her eyes were shut; she had gone into coma. There had been no pain, Tony said, nothing to speak of. No warning. Just sudden panic in the night, as if she were coming apart inside; and she called his name, asking him to hold her safe. Perhaps that was all he should have done; and forgotten help.

The doctor, who came soon, suggested some haemorrhage. A part of Rose had just grown quiet and quit the contest, since she herself was unwilling. Tony and I were soon in the back of the ambulance with Rose, travelling to hospital. Her breathing was faint; her eyes never opened. After that, in hospital, it was only a matter of how long other things took to give up; she lived hour after hour, technically at least. I sat beside Tony, sometimes with arm around him. A nurse brought tea and biscuits. Morning, grey then bright, burst against the windows.

Tony grieved hugely, and at last quite gently, as she fled her flesh. After a time he rose with dignity, placed his hand on her cooling brow, and said, 'She's all right now, isn't she? Say she is.'

'She's all right now, Tony.'

'It wasn't for nothing, was it?'

'Never. It made all the sense in the world.'

'We have to believe that, don't we?'

'I expect we do.'

'Then help me,' he asked.

I tried. My fervent best. And if that wasn't convincing enough, at least I was capable of calling a cab and helping him from the hospital. Back at his house, I dosed him liberally with whisky and called an undertaker to make arrangements.

'You don't mind sitting with me for a while?' Tony asked.

'Of course not.' I could think of more difficult demands.

'I'd just like to talk about Rose, mostly.'

'Yes.'

'And me.'

'Yes.'

'It won't add up.'

'It will,' I argued. 'It must.'

'You're not just saying that?'

'I'm not just saying anything. You're talking, remember, not me. So try.'

He did, in his wandering way, with no small success. And by noon he had subsided into drunken sleep. I felt able to leave him, then, to walk down the hill and set my own house in order.

That problem, it seemed, was no longer so great. For only Terror inhabited it now. Irene had gone neatly, dishes washed and bed made. Outside, under the lean-to, her last pieces lay smashed on the ground. On the wheel there was just the one-line note: 'I have to believe I can find what I need.' The quiet was stunning. Until Terror, unfed, gave a whimper. So I tried to get on with it and filled his food bowl. All loss seemed one and I had no undertaker to call. Finally I went back up through the fern and borrowed a bottle of Tony's whisky from his cabinet while he slept.

In the end, numbed by the night, bruised by the bottle, I slept too. I woke towards evening, in some queer half light, and dawdled disoriented through the house until memory began to fall like brick after solid brick around me, trapping me with the truth; I was alone again. I might have offered myself music as orientation. Instead, with leaden legs, I climbed the hill to see to Tony, and cook him food.

Later that evening, with funeral fixed, Rose's remote relatives rallied, and whisky again warm in my gut, I descended towards the silence of my own house. There was music elsewhere, though; I could hear the tribal tom-toms across the trees. I staggered unsteadily at the door, and fell inside. Terror made a whine of surprise or sympathy and licked my face as I lay there. Possibly I called someone's name for human help. It was evidently not forthcoming, nor any other. Since I soon seemed unbroken, I revived and limped through the house, finally sitting at this desk to summon sense. Until the silence became a protective thing. Impeccable, quite without flaw.

December 31, 1899: I sit here sleepless perhaps for the last time & wait for the chime of the Timepiece on the mantel to tell me my business with this Century is done & that in truth I live a New. Florence has no patience with such Sentimentality & has long retired to bed. It is just a Night, she says, just another Night & there will be mouths again to feed tomorrow & all the Tasks of living. I cannot doubt she speaks truth & yet I sit here all the same this Journal on my knee so that those chimes shall not take me by Surprise & so that I shall have some hand to hold to should memories shake me in the moment they come. A hand? Whose? It is done now, this Century & most of my Life & I need suffer no further fancies & failures. For I may soon be free. All I need do is watch the hour advance, hear the chime, & would that I could clothe myself Clean in a new Century.

*   *   *

171

Indeed; he appeared to have done that with some spectacular success. For, as family tradition arranged the tale, he was never seen beyond that evening; he wandered off alone into the twentieth century. Grandmother found his celibate bed unoccupied, searched the place without avail, called brothers from a neighbouring valley, organised a search party. But they failed to find even footprints where he had gone. They dragged in the river, searched the beach below. Nothing. None saw where he had departed in his sixty-fourth year; no countryman, no townsman. He had dispersed from the land like smoke in high wind. I can imagine them calling his name in places high and low, and only echoes calling back. What I cannot imagine is where he went, where he wandered to the last. Through forsaken gumfield, ransacked goldfield, fallen forests, or to Mary's grave? His undiscovered journal might have given his hunters clue, but his favoured floorboard was never lifted in their time, and some years later he was declared officially and safely dead. Until recent renovation brought his life to light again.

I begin to wish it hadn't been. I begin to wish he'd stuck with his own century, and left mine alone. Get the hell back, old man. Get the hell back where you belong.

Morning finds my music after all. The day is cool; I can't complain.

14

March 21:

THE DAYS DIMINISH; WE ARE HALF WAY TO WINTER. ROSE IS five days buried, and Tony survives alone. The past week, until today's devastation, has not been rich in remarkable event. Tony talks about selling out and leaving. 'It's not the same,' he tells me. 'My heart's not in it.' For he has tried, ineffectually, to clear Rose's garden of weeds, for another start. I tell him to try in spring. He is drinking hard, mostly alone; his heart will likely not last to spring.

Visitors. Tom Hyde with news of a protest meeting, Rangiwai's largest yet, to demand halt on plans for filling the estuary. 'We're over the top,' he said with glee. 'This is just to clinch it. The coup de grace.' I did my best to give him some attention.
  'That girl you had here,' he added obscurely. 'She gone?'
  'Yes.'
  'Sorry if I sound inquisitive. It's just that I thought I saw her the other day. It puzzled me.'
  'Oh?'

'Up the road, at Daniels' place. I didn't think she looked the happiest.'

Janet. She had complimentary tickets for Anna's opening night. No need to ask with whose compliments. 'I think you should go along with me,' she said. 'It wouldn't hurt, would it?'

'Consider you might be wrong.'

'Come on, Paul; please.'

'Tell me the rest of the scenario. Her dressing room afterwards? A drink or two?'

'Only if you want to. Please come anyway.'

'I'm sorry. No.'

'I'm sorry too,' she said.

'Leave an empty seat. I'll be there in spirit.'

She didn't think I meant it. She drove away.

First I tried the estuary; I put out the mullet net and swam. Each time, now, could be the last. The last of the mullet; the last swim of summer. For the days are swiftly cooling now. I left the water shivering, or perhaps still just shaky. Too marginal to say.

Then I tried this desk. But there was no conversation left, no consolation, just silence on the other side. Where in hell was he, then?

Finally the lean-to. And I found something there. I found, in fact, a large clump of clay spinning larger in my hands. I began to find my biggest bloody pot ever. I couldn't believe it, and then I could. For I waited for the clay to quit, my hands to say no, and waited in vain. Even the shell declined to give or split as I pushed my arm full length within to spread it finer, that slender skin to the limit of its possibility. Old man, I think I hear you clear. And your poor Mary. Do you meet where all is Music & Light perpetual? Or might you, like those broken earthbound souls of forest trees whose proud flesh is long Dust, be excavated tediously, by someone you cannot guess or imagine, & when Scraped & Cleaned shine out with the mystery of what you were & are. Rose & Tony too.

Was that the message? Anyway it helped. In the end the bloody thing just sat there singing. My knees felt weak; the sweat dripped. I fell trembling on a stool & took comfort in tobacco & tried to look at it longer. It was no explanation, of course. And might never find function. Just clay shaped to human need: just dream, not hope; just love, not lust; just a whisper, not a cry. For what we were & are. God forgive lovers all.

Or someone.

For after I regained some semblance of sanity, found myself less giddy on my feet, I carried that fantasy carefully to the drying room; and discovered the day fast darkening. It seemed I'd forgotten my net, and the tide was issuing out of the estuary. I walked down to the water, through the dusk, among the trees, until sand was shifting underfoot and the sea rising chilly about my legs. In the murky light I groped towards the pale flash of fish imprisoned in the mesh, and found the net still remarkably heavy as I freed them into my bag. Towards the centre of the net, it appeared, there was some obstruction, some snag, perhaps a drifted branch or log, holding it all down. I waded towards it gingerly in the gloom, lest a stingray flap and poisonously lash my legs, but it was nothing so hazardous. Just shapeless and soft. Streaming hair; a bundle of garments and flesh. I lifted the face free of sea, but some hours late. Irene quite harmless. Irene quite dead.

On the beach, though, I performed passionate acts of resurrection, trying to empty her lungs, kissing her fervently, forcing warm air between her cold lips. She refused to live, to breathe again, within my embrace; she had found a track to follow, and grown solid in the sea. So finally I separated my salty mouth from hers, and carried her away, Terror whimpering at my heel, up the hill to the house she had so late and loveless inhabited. And so thin and emptied now. The pity, then: to waste the world when it's all we have; perhaps all such wild words, in the end, were just hostage to despair. I placed her lightly on my couch, and the sea dripped down from her dress in puddles on my floor, and became shallowly creeping tide across the room. Then I went up to Tony's to call the police, so they could take charge of my problem, in accord with civilised custom; and they came soon to take Irene away. With questions, of course. Questions I didn't doubt were just beginning.

So now they are gone, I sit here and experiment with one myself. It is not unfamiliar. Why. Which at length turns out to be the answer too.

15

March 24:

QUESTIONS; MORE QUESTIONS. I SPIN AMONG THEM, A TWIG on a tide. The detective sergeant in charge of the affair is a bulky, laboured man seemingly distracted by domesticity; his wife calls frequently on his office phone. It seems possible, from his often desperate replies, that she may be suffering menopausal crisis of some kind. To give him his due, he seems to sense or fairly allow that we all have problems. Which doesn't mean he is slow to test my guard.

For example, 'The pathologist's report says she was filled to the gills on drugs. Would you know anything about that?'

'Nothing,' I insisted.

To check this, then, they proceeded to pry my house apart. They looked under lampshades, peered into pots, groped into gloomy corners. No drugs.

'Let's go through it again,' he said later. 'How long did this kid live with you?'

'Three or four months,' I replied.

Which was what I had told him twice.

'And you haven't seen her in how long?'

'Two or three weeks.'

His past notes confirmed this; he tried fresh tack. 'You were never high, the two of you, when she was with you?'

'If you mean on pot or pills, no. On other things, perhaps.'

'Oh?' He was interested now. 'Tell me more.'

'On clay now and then.'

'Clay?'

'A dangerous drug; toxic in overdose. You should have it on your list.'

'Don't put me on.'

'I can even give you the name of the pusher. He's said to breathe on it first. Hence the toxic content.'

'Look, Mr. Pike, we just want the truth.'

'I'm trying.' Perhaps I was.

'You told me she worked with you for a while. What more was she?'

'I think that's my business, unless you're pressing a charge.'

He put on a worldly face. 'Just a stray fuck, was she?'

'Is that the charge?'

'Come on, now. If you assist our inquiries in a reasonable manner, we can assume you have nothing to hide.'

'I plead guilty to stray fucking, then. I've been in the grip of the vile habit all my adult life. There. Nothing hidden. Perhaps it calls for psychiatric help.'

'She shared your bed.' He decided he could afford to be formal.

'Yes. That's all.' For it had to be now.

'Why did she leave? Did you fight, quarrel?'

'No fight, no quarrel. She just left.'

'Why?'

'She doubtless had a reason.'

'Because you refused to accept responsibility?'

'For the way things are, yes.'

'I mean for her condition.'

'She was in a fairly sad state when she came. I did my best.'

'I'm talking about when she left. Her condition when she left.'

I failed to understand, and possibly showed this.

'Come on, now. You're not going to tell me you didn't know she was pregnant. I won't wear that.' And, to prove the point, he pushed the pathologist's report towards me. 'Near twelve weeks, he says.'

He watched my face, and believed me after all.

The house is hellish quiet. The police car has returned me here and again departed. Perhaps for Daniels' den; they may have additional information more innocently to offer. But I had more than enough. For if love and lust had indistinguishable consequence, what then was the name of the game? Life, no more and no less; and that to be played diversely to the death. And as I passed pictures in the gallery it was less Anna's hand I searched to hold than sweet Charlie's now. The couch where Irene lay is still stained, slow to dry. And the big pot, despite all, has gone into the biscuit kiln. Also I feel like fire myself on so cold a night; as I begin to shiver I gather logs in the grate, setting them alight and taking the comfort I can from the warmth of flame on the flesh. Then I sit at this desk to nourish the delusion that there are yet accounts to be kept, books to be balanced.

16

April 1:

ALL FOOLS' DAY; I CAN CALL IT MY OWN. AND A SPARKLING
Saturday, it seemed. A bracing day for Tom's mass meeting.
Earlier, he threatened to collect me and take me in his car, but
I told him no. Yet escape wasn't so easy. Tony turned up
instead. I had been to open the kiln, the main one; just the one
pot sat there reverberant, glowing with green glaze. And, satis-
fied with that survival, I had gone down into my neglected
garden to salvage the last edible things of summer and dig in
the rest. Tony, of course, insisted we should show our faces at
the meeting; he persuaded me along in muddy boots, and we
stood at the outskirts of the thickening crowd. Wild-haired
Tom grabbed the microphone with gusto, to the manner born,
led cheers and chants, while the colourful young circulated with
bold banners. More sober citizens of Rangiwai applauded respectably at the rear. Among them doubtless were the dapperly
dressed developers of whom Tom had spoken, possibly even
the prospective pioneers of the new peninsula. The estuary was

bright with tide beyond the makeshift platform. The mangroves, crisp with autumnal light, were indifferent to the human storm. Speeches thundered and crackled and whined through the creaky public address system; the greenly garbed hills gave back confused echoes as planners and bureaucrats, all manner of malevolent men, were shredded and pulverised and recycled. There was the sting of triumph in the day. None could doubt the battle won.

Then Daniels rose, in haphazardly flashy raiment. Spokesman, prophet for the young. Guardian of the future's virtue. He had, like me, cleanly cruised through police inquiry; but he had, unlike me, not been at the graveside after Irene's tearfully perplexed parents claimed her body back for burial. Then again, I had no sufficient reason to expect him there; I hardly expected myself there. And fled before my hand was taken, or anyone obliged me to account for my presence; there had been no more than a dozen mourners, and the clergyman momentarily forgot her name.

That was some yesterdays gone. Today was Daniels with flourish of arms, passionate pleas to preserve the magic of God's green earth. He appeared soon to be embracing his summation.

At first I thought I hadn't heard right. Then I knew I had. 'It's a pity,' he cried, 'to waste the world when it's all we have.' And flew down from the platform upon the applause.

Irene had never even owned that much as epitaph. After all.

'Come on,' I said to Tony. 'I've wasted enough.'

Home again, I found Janet had made another call; a note thrust under the door. 'Think about tonight again,' she scrawled. 'Please come. Will wait for you outside ticket box until five minutes before time.'

I didn't compost the paper on which the words were written, not right away. I sat, drank, and considered. Until there was no longer need. Until evening. Terror made noises to be fed then, so I did that before I left, and shut him in the house.

At the theatre the crowd had gone, the doors were shut. There was the predictable grey gnome on guard behind the counter at the stage door; I gave him my huge parcel. 'I want Mrs. Pike to get this at the end,' I told him.

'No message?' he said. 'Who from?'

'Her husband. She'll know.'

'No flowers?'

'No flowers. Just this.'

'I hope it's not a bloody bomb,' he observed.

'Take the wrapping off, if you like.'

He was content to pull back paper and peer inside.

'It seems all right.' he said uncertainly.

'I just don't want it broken,' I said. 'That's all. I'd like it in her dressing room at the end, if you can manage it.' I pushed a couple of dollars into his hand, and began to turn away.

Too late, though. I froze before I could flee. For within the theatre the sound of the orchestra diminished, and there was Anna's voice distinct. Into the recitative before the first aria. Waiting to tryst with Edgardo in the garden. And then the aria. Regnava nel silenzio; a glimpse of the ghost of a murdered girl. The voice was there still. True, with less shimmer. But the legato line gracefully under control as she told her heart, still filled with love for Edgardo. With cavatina past, the first cadenza was the test now, the first cabaletta. Not a taxing one, not yet, but the coloratura was still there, it seemed; still there. I could breathe, if not too amply. For if she were to tire, and the years tell their tale, it would be after the bridging recitative, and into the second round of the cabaletta, the fast one. Quando rapito in estasi; the joy, the ecstasy, the dizzy spiralling of spirit. I could believe it then. For there was no fatigue and little loss. All that was left to learn was whether she would try for a high D, to climax the cabaletta, or let it pass. The choice was hers; the gamble. The orchestra lifted and she seemed to sense the possibility, then richly the fact; and that tender triumph was hers. She had it made again. She was free.

'Go farther up the stairs if you like,' said the generous gnome behind me. 'Closer. Stay quiet; no one will notice you.'

But I preferred not to wait upon Edgardo's entrance. I didn't know that I cared for the sound of a tenor, or the duet. I had enough to last.

I walked, and kept walking. One block and then another; and perhaps the same block again. When I got back to the theatre the doors were shut once more upon the second act.

'What is it now?' said the gnome. 'Forget something?'

'That pot.' It still sat bulky behind his counter. 'You'll make sure she gets it?'

'Of course I'll bloody make sure. It's in my way here.'

'And be careful.'

'You said that.'

'It's important.'

'So I see.'

Another couple of dollars pushed in his hand made him less querulous. 'You can still go up if you like,' he said.

It seemed I meant to, anyway, for the mad scene. Otherwise I was there on pathetic pretext. I went quickly up the stairs, and moved unchallenged into the murk of the wings. The chorus had just quietened with horror, the wedding celebration stilled, while Lucia drifted madly down the stairs from her unchosen bridal chamber, splashed with blood, dagger in hand, bridegroom slain, and outcast Edgardo forever beyond her now. People shaded my view of the scene. No matter; her sound was sufficient. More. She didn't take the conventional cadenzas; she had her own to put herself freshly on test. And still more stamina to show. For she didn't succumb to the pyrotechnics Donizetti proposed; she unravelled the possibilities for her own intricate purpose, let them fly free and gathered them back again, first in trickles, then in tempests, until all grief and madness ebbed away between the risen reefs of love and death. I needed no convincing that she would find the E flat she was looking for, on the last cabaletta, as she fell in fatal swoon. That long and luminous sound followed me as I departed down the stairs, past the nodding gnome, before applause began to slam up out of the auditorium. I might be free too.

More so than I knew. For Daniels had chosen that day for his descent, or some of his vengeful tribesmen. Perhaps I'd enraged them by my absence. They had smashed most of what they could smash in the house, torn what they could tear, and left the walls dense with wild graffiti. Some required translation, but the general themes were clear. I was a murdering bastard. A clapped out cop-out. An agent of the fuzz. In short, a shit.

I had no inclination to protest their verdict. Then I remembered Terror. My guardian. Had he, after all, let it happen?

I called and whistled. No response, no wet rush through the fern, no bark, no wagging tail. So with a torch I looked outside. And finally found him under a shrub, bashed and bleeding, but breathing still. I gathered him up, carried him inside, and nursed him as life left. The blood ran in rivulets through my clothing, down my skin, stickily clotting. I took the last of Tony's whisky as he died, as the blood diminished, and drifted into kind of dream. It appeared I was in some wild waltz with Mary Dennis, in cascades of confusing music, and the sequins on her dark dress lived with light while her pale face remained as remote as on that day of her death; she declined all speech as I fought feverishly to chat her up. Then I understood why. It wasn't so much that I was naked. It was the grotesque growth of hair the length of my body; even my hands were hirsute. The hairy man himself, the animal unashamed, on that madman's mission. So I woke to morning, the debris and damage vivid around, and a dead dog coldly clutched in my arms, and after a time walked dizzily into the day. I dug a deep hole for Terror beneath a tree, a much favoured pissing place, and covered him with care. Back in the house I made small attempt to set things right, beside pushing upright this toppled desk, and hunting out some fresh clothes. I would that I could clothe myself Clean in a new Century.

17

April ?:

IT SEEMS I HAVE FOLLOWED THE SUN HERE & PERHAPS SUMMER
as it flees towards another Hemisphere. For I felt Winter behind me, making steady advance up this narrow Land, as I
drove always in northerly direction & always with Dust & sunlight obscuring my vision. Here I find myself almost at Land's
end, nothing but vast Expanse of Pacific ocean beyond, & I
think this journeying now finished & Winter still not far behind
me now. Nor my Life as it has been lived. I do not care to
think about it much & yet it seems I must if I am to make full
Account. The waves beat tumultuous tattoo on this long Sandy
shore which soars into far haze & pale Sunlight so far as the
eye can see; it is a pathway without Visible end & in the tradition of the old Maories of this Land the track by which Dead
Souls travel before they deliver themselves from the Earth by
leap into the underworld. I thus find it more sufficient to my
Purpose than any other place to pause & perhaps still more so
as my eye lifts again & again to consider this long curve of
coast all Desert & deserted & where the footprints of a man

solitary can reverberate in the Wilderness before tides & winds remove them. I find no grief in the fact but rather the taut Truth which man must embrace at his hazard & then go on because he must. For Death is a lean feast for hungry lovers & Life is the only Dance we have hope to learn & as we shuffle imperfectly through our paces because needs must then we know . . . Know? We know nothing. We trust, if we can. And if we can't, we make do. The rhythms of the Dance ask no understanding.

Already Rangiwai is remote. The developers & speculators & hippies & elegant executives could battle for the peninsula to their purposes now & when all Dust & Dialogue is done & the inevitable encountered there will be no room, in that tidy Museum, for hairy men or the likes of Pike. So I farewelled it, after all, without Pain too great, after last walk along the Estuary shore & then shutting the house & filling the claypit perversely with mostly broken pots & things of plastic manufacture doubtless to confuse some future Archaeologist who may see some merit & even much virtue in contemplation of men of my Century, God knows why, for all that cripples can tell him; a Century in which man could mistake himself as God, for lack of any other. When I had covered the pit, to provide for that contingency, I found I had inexplicably overlooked one good pot remaining. Why that survival & not another? I took it without ceremony & threw it high through the trees & heard it falling & shattering on the shore below. The sound was altogether satisfying & pleasing to my sense of the random. For if none can choose, all are chosen. The Agent in whose hands I placed the Property before my Departure might have agreed, yes, it is all but a Business Proposition & needed no Gospel to quote in support, for Why Not, that is the Way of things now. We are not here, he might have said with his fast talk, to make Friends, but to Buy & Sell. For what he did say, in Truth, was that he saw no Problem, none at all, in finding willing Buyers at far above the price I sought & was

187

amazed to find I should think to sell so cheaply. The art in
Selling, so he said, was to ask the highest price Buyers could
pay. But that price, I told him, could be too high. He did not
see fit to take my Meaning. Look, he said. Look, Mr Pike, you
just leave it to me, I'll see you right. And slapped my shoulder
in heavy good Humour. So perhaps the true Art of Selling is
to allow others to fix the price they think can be willingly paid
& have no Pretty Conscience about the consequence, for Why
Not, that is just Land the man wants to sell, not my Life, &
I am Fool to think otherwise & inhabit Confusion just when I
think myself Free & no more than an emptied cage of skin &
bone looking for tidier tenant than it had until such time as it
is condemned as Slum Residence & judged unfit for human
occupation. Judged, though, by whom? Sentence was long
since passed. A life sentence, with but one large Privilege to
pass the prisoner's time, or torment him, as the case may be.
Love. Eros & Agape of the ancients; either or both, most in-
timately intertwined. Ask why & one finds the judge who
passed sentence long departed, before one could glimpse his
Face. Some claim to recall him, but the particulars they offer
as to his Appearance & Nature are too diverse & confusing &
contradictory to be useful & leave this Matter more inscrutable
& indecipherable than ever. Would that it all were but the
Farce some now see, as light Entertainment to follow their
Wining & Dining & otherwise Decorative pursuits. For the
Scenery has plainly been arranged with great Patience & Care
& no small Sensitivity & it is a pity the same attention was not
given the Script, which lacks Credibility, Consistency & Coher-
ence & provides for so large & confusing & implausible a cast
of characters. Nevertheless, one could critically add that the
project is as Ambitious as it is Ambiguous, & it may be that
so imaginative & untidily fertile an Author will have more to
say. It may also be just a matter of finding my own place in
the Script, but for the moment the Prompt Box is empty, unless
those waves beating at the edge of my Vision are in Truth

seeking to distract my Attention for more than ordinary Purpose & telling me that the Loose End upon which I swing will yet find its place in a meticulous Tapestry. That all life, love & death, in whatever capricious convolution, will yet make some serene Sense.

I made no human farewell, unless to that Agent; I departed swiftly & mercifully, in fairness to Survivors. Not that there were lives to be breached in consequence of that Departure; no longer. So I drove, through Dust & along mostly empty Highway, into peaceful places where Summer more lengthily lingered, & finally found myself here, with no further to travel & too little to tell. I parked where the hills of this Land slump to the sea, the Clay to the Sands, & where there were but few drab human dwellings scattered in the thin Sunlight of late Afternoon. It was as likely a Refuge as any other. Bulldozers had recently cut a road close under the Hills & as I walked a little way, seeking path to the Shore, I fingered the clay which had spilled down. Pale stuff, not altogether unpromising to my Purpose, perhaps with Experiment, & with distinct fresh odour of its own. I could not deny some small stir of interest in its Prospects. But such interest could wait until I saw, at least, just where I had arrived. I clambered down to the shore in the fading Afternoon & the crisp Sand, washed by Tide and dried by Sun, crackled underfoot as I trod it. The long beach was vastly Vacant, as if at Time's end too, apart from a sturdy Maorie & his son who were trying to draw a net through the waves. The child was small & soon I perceived in Difficulties on his end of the net. So rather than consider the Sun as it sank red on the Horizon I felt myself obliged to offer such assistance as I could render. For there was no loss in drenching my dusty clothes. The child gratefully gave up the pole he held, his Father acknowledging my arrival with friendly enough wave before we proceeded to drag the heavy net through the Surf, with no small struggle. At the end of the effort we had an impressive selection of fish fluttering on the sands. While the child gathered them into a large flaxen kit, the Maorie & I at last had chance to converse in agreeable & then most amiable manner. At length it seemed this saturated stranger from nowhere called Paul Pike had earned himself invitation to eat, also a bed for the Night or longer if he wished, & we three walked the huge shore together, our footprints mingled, in the Last of the light.

So then. Get on with the Dance. Clap & chant & stamp. Love & laugh & weep. Sing out, if you must. If you don't, then have mercy on those who do & take pity on those who can't. It is our furious & fatally human Fever to know our clay as faultily fired & mortally flawed. Be gentle with strangers & forgive lovers all. For tomorrow we live.